C 990 006 093 459 DC

CH00621320

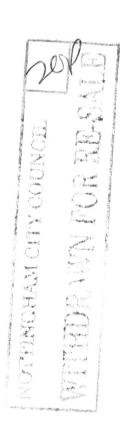

NOTTINGHAM CITY COUNCIL

WITHDRAWN FOR RE-SALE

20p

The Hunting Trip

The Hunting Trip

STEVEN GRAY

A Black Horse Western

ROBERT HALE · LONDON

© Steven Gray 1999
First published in Great Britain 1999

ISBN 0 7090 6546 9

Robert Hale Limited
Clerkenwell House
Clerkenwell Green
London EC1R 0HT

The right of Steven Gray to be identified as
author of this work has been asserted by him
in accordance with the Copyright, Designs and
Patents Act 1988.

NOTTINGHAM CITY COUNCIL	
Morley Books	19.1.00
	£10.25

Photoset in North Wales by
Derek Doyle & Associates, Mold, Flintshire.
Printed and bound in Great Britain by
WBC Book Manufacturers Limited, Bridgend.

One

Veronica MacLean made sure the two horses in the corral had enough feed and water to last them the day. Satisfied, she stood by the split rail fence, lifting her face to the sun, thinking about all the tasks needing to be done.

Her father and two elder brothers were away, driving the cattle to market on the far side of the mountains, and her mother was busy with the never-ending household chores. So Veronica, at nineteen, had been deemed old enough to be left in charge of the ranch. She was determined nothing should go wrong.

'Ronny!' Calling to her from the house, her mother interrupted her thoughts. 'Dinner's almost ready. Come on in and wash up.'

'OK, Ma, coming.' Veronica paused to take one more look round. She sighed. How she loved it out here. How she loved the ranch.

She might not have felt quite so happy had she known she was being watched from the nearby hillside.

'What d'you think?' Mick Crowell looked at his two companions. 'Do we go on down and rob the place or not?'

'The women are alone,' Hal Hatcher objected. 'It don't seem right to me.'

Crowell sighed heavily. He, Hal and Bruce Norton had been friends for years. They called themselves the Crowell Gang: 'Crowell' because Mick, at twenty-five, was the oldest by six months; 'gang' because they were outlaws.

But not very successful ones. They might be wanted by the law, with prices on their heads, but instead of having stolen money lining their pockets, they were more often, like now, down on their luck.

It was because the small ranch was deserted, except for two women, and so should prove easy pickings, Crowell had suggested robbing it in the first place.

Norton hesitated before saying, 'I know robbing women ain't right, Hal, but we ain't got no money or supplies. It ain't like we're goin' to hurt 'em or nothin'.'

'I should hope not,' Crowell said.

'Oh, OK.' Hatcher, persuaded, agreed reluctantly.

The ranch was well looked after. The buildings – house, barn, worksheds – kept in good repair. Wood was stacked against one wall of the house. The two horses were sturdy and well groomed.

Hoping to have surprise on their side, they dismounted by the corral, approaching the house on foot. Drawing their guns they reached the porch with no sign of movement or discovery from inside.

It all went wrong as Crowell stepped on to the porch. The door opened and the girl they had watched earlier came out. Close up they saw she was very pretty, with long brown hair loosely tied back from her face, and brown eyes. And the man's shirt and old skirt she wore didn't detract from her good figure either.

Everyone came to a halt, looking at one another in shock.

Although it had never touched her, Veronica was aware that living out here on a lonely ranch, with no near neighbours, violence was never far away. By themselves she and her mother were particularly vulnerable.

Quickly she took in the appearance of the three young men – lean, hard faces, untidy hair, unshaven chins. With their guns out and pointed, they looked guilty and meant trouble!

'Ma!' she screamed and went to run back into the house.

'Oh hell,' Crowell muttered, leaping towards her.

She almost managed to slam the door in his face. But he kicked it back against the wall, at the same time grabbing her around the waist, manhandling her into the hall beyond.

Struggling uselessly in Crowell's grasp, Veronica screamed again. A door further down the hall opened and a woman wearing an apron came into view.

'Ronny, what . . . oh my God!' Mrs MacLean raised flour-covered hands to her cheeks, staring in horror at this invasion of her home.

Crowell yelled, 'Get her!'

Before Norton or Hatcher could move, the woman dived back into the kitchen. And crying out, 'Let me go!' Veronica kicked Mick hard and painfully on the shin.

'Ow!' He shoved her away from him.

As she thumped heavily against the wall, Mrs MacLean stepped out into the hall. She had a shotgun in her hands.

Screaming, 'Look out, Ronny!', she pulled the trigger letting fly with both barrels.

Crowell, Hatcher, Norton and Veronica all dived to the floor as the buckshot exploded into the ceiling, sending plaster showering over them.

'Jesus Christ!' Crowell said, his heart thumping. He grabbed at Veronica as she tried to squirm away from him.

Before Mrs MacLean could reload, Norton jumped up and ran to her, dragging the shotgun from her grasp, clutching her arm.

'Don't you dare hurt my mother! Leave her alone!'

'We don't mean any harm,' Hatcher said, thinking this wasn't exactly going the way they'd planned. 'We don't wanna hurt anyone.'

'My friend's right,' Crowell said breathlessly, pulling Veronica to her feet. ♠

But as he was pointing his gun at both women, Mrs MacLean felt justified in saying, 'It looks like it! How dare you come in here, attacking my daughter, threatening us?'

'I'm sorry,' Crowell said, feeling a bit helpless. 'If you promise to behave yourselves, I promise we'll put our guns away.' He nodded at Hal and Bruce to do so.

'I suppose we have little alternative.'

'What do you want?' Veronica demanded.

'Any money you've got in the house . . .'

'Well, you'll be unlucky there! My father's away selling our cattle. He left us with just a few dollars for emergencies. And we had to spend some of that on supplies.'

'Miss, you won't find anyone in more need of emergency help than us. And ma'am,' Crowell looked at Mrs

8

MacLean, 'you seem to be in the middle of cooking dinner. We wouldn't mind feeding.'

'For goodness sake.'

'No, Ronny, it's all right. Let's give these men what they want so they can be on their way without hurting us. You won't hurt us, will you?'

'No, ma'am, I said we wouldn't. I give you my word. We're thieves, we ain't nothin' else. We wouldn't be doing this lessen it was necessary. And we wanna be on our way the same as you wanna be rid of us. So Bruce and Hal will go with you, see what there is to eat, while you, miss, mebbe you'd show me where this money for emergencies is.'

'Ronny, will you be all right?' Mrs MacLean asked anxiously, not wanting to let her daughter out of her sight.

'Of course I will.' But while Veronica sounded scornful she was still scared, not sure whether she could trust these men to keep their word.

With Crowell still holding her arm, she led the way into the tiny room her father proudly called his office.

'It's in the desk.'

'Get it then.'

Veronica's heart missed several beats as she went over to the desk. Her father kept a loaded gun in the top drawer. Could she – dare she – get hold of it? Would going for a gun only provoke the men into a violence they said they didn't intend?

She glanced up. Crowell had wandered over to the window and was looking out of it. Taking no notice of her. Trembling she opened the drawer, hand reaching for the Colt.

'Don't try it!' Crowell was suddenly by her side. He slammed the drawer shut, nearly trapping her fingers.

With a little squeal, Veronica jumped back.

'Don't be stupid. Everything's OK ain't it? Why don't you believe me when I say we ain't gonna hurt you?'

'All right,' Veronica mumbled. 'The money's in the bottom drawer.'

Unfortunately the amount was disappointing. Just two dollars and a few cents. Still, beggars could hardly be choosers and Crowell pocketed it gratefully.

'Let's go back to your ma. See if dinner is ready. It smells real good.'

Veronica took no notice of this flattery.

Even so Mick decided to try and be friendly. After all, she was pretty and it wasn't often he had the chance to meet nice girls.

'Ronny is an unusual name ain't it?'

'It's short for Veronica.' She made him sound like an idiot for not realizing the fact. 'What's yours?'

'I don't think you need to know that.'

Two

Zachary Cobb sat upright on the train seat, staring out of the window, a scowl on his face. Beyond, the scenery flashed by: lush meadows, hills covered with pine-trees, a glimpse now and then of a river, its blue matching that of the clear sky. He took none of it in. He was thinking, 'Why me?'

Two days earlier, Mr Bellington had summoned him to his luxurious office in St Louis and said, 'My dear nephew, my sister's son, Lambert, wishes to go on a hunting expedition to Wyoming. He particularly wants to shoot a buffalo, while there are still some left to shoot. Mr Cobb, I want you to accompany him, make sure no harm comes to him and ensure he gets his own way.'

Cobb shifted uncomfortably in the chair. He was a private detective, good at what he did, not a nursemaid. To accompany a young man on a hunting trip was beneath him and his abilities. Moreover he'd heard enough stories about Lambert Hutchinson's behaviour that he wasn't exactly enamoured with the boy's reputation. Neither did he like or approve of hunting for hunting's sake.

11

But when Mr Bellington said, 'Is that all right?' he swallowed his pride and raised no argument.

Working for Bellington's Private Detective Agency meant doing what Mr Bellington wanted, resigning or being fired. Mostly Cobb liked his work and had no desire to quit it. But he wasn't happy.

Sitting opposite, watching anxiously, Neil Travis knew Cobb was in a bad mood. What he didn't know was whether he was going to get into trouble over it. As Cobb had mentioned something about being tired of spoiled and stupid young men, Neil rather feared the worst.

Nervously he cleared his throat and spoke for the first time since they'd caught the train. 'How much longer before we reach Cypress Grove?'

Cobb dragged his eyes away from the window. He grimaced on looking at Neil, said abruptly, 'An hour or so,' and went back to his moody contemplation of the view.

The two of them made strange companions.

Cobb was twenty-nine and had been a lawman before being recruited to work for Bellington's Agency. Proud of himself and his position, he dressed neatly, wearing dark suits over white shirts, and he was clean-shaven, his dark brown hair cut short.

Neil was a thief. Some months before when he saved Cobb's life, Cobb said he could stop being an outlaw and partner him. An offer Cobb immediately regretted. Mr Bellington would most certainly not approve if he ever found out. And at twenty-one, Neil had brown hair hanging below his shoulders, was trying to grow a moustache and wore exceedingly casual clothes. Cobb

12

thought he was bad for the image the detective agency tried to promote.

Later Cobb said, 'When we meet Lambert Hutchinson . . .'

'Lambert?' Neil interrupted with a little laugh. 'That's a funny name ain't it?'

Cobb frowned in annoyance. 'It's a family name on Mr Bellington's side. Listen to me, Lambert is the son of a bank's president and comes from New York. He is very important and very rich, so I want you to be on your best behaviour. No swearing or saying "ain't".'

That, Neil decided, would be difficult: he did both naturally, without thought.

'And while you're at it you can get yourself some decent clothes. And a haircut.'

'You ain't being fair.' Neil lapsed into unhappy silence.

Naturally Cobb had to have the last word. 'And remind me later when there's time to lecture you on not being disrespectful about a client.'

'Your bath is ready, sir.'

Lambert Hutchinson looked up from the local newspaper he was reading. Not that it contained much of interest – mostly reports to do with cattle and their prices.

'Thank you, Gifford. Afterwards I shall rest for the afternoon so I am refreshed for this evening. And while I'm bathing lay out my best suit. Make sure it has no creases in it. Mr Cobb is arriving on the afternoon train and I want to make a good impression.'

'Yes, sir. I'm sure you will, sir.'

13

'So am I. And ensure Quinn and Beaumont go to meet the train.'

Towel, soap and hot water awaited Lambert in the hotel's one bathroom. Undressing, he studied himself in the mirror, approving wholeheartedly of what he saw.

He was tall and lean, with a good figure that his expensive clothes made the most of. He had neatly cut, black, wavy hair and blue eyes, which he believed was a fatally attractive combination to the ladies.

As the only son after five girls, he had always been thoroughly spoiled: denied nothing, with servants to do everything for him. The best of schooling. Money. If challenged about his way of life, Lambert would have felt most surprised that anyone should think it could be otherwise.

Relaxing in the bath he realized how much he was looking forward to this hunting trip. He was the first member of the family to visit the West. He'd have so much to tell them about its quaint customs and the quaint people.

He'd just celebrated his twentieth birthday. This expedition was the present for which he'd asked his parents. Somewhat to his surprise they had agreed to it, for usually they treated him as if he was still a baby and had to be protected.

Moreover, it was the first holiday he'd ever taken on his own. Well, not on his own exactly – Mr Cobb and Gifford would be with him, and the bank's vice-president would be waiting in Cypress Grove for his return – but at least the first holiday without his parents fussing around him, telling him what he could and could not do.

It would give him the chance to prove to his father how capable he was, a child no longer. On his return to New York he could assume his rightful position of importance at the bank.

As he had no doubt he would make a success of banking, he also had no doubt Mr Cobb, a westerner, would be most impressed with how he, an easterner, rode and shot game and handled himself. How could it be otherwise?

Maurice Hutchinson, President of the First Presidential Bank of New York, sat in his comfortable leather chair behind his large oak desk, in his oak-lined office. A pile of papers awaited his attention. Being in charge of such a substantial and famous financial institution meant a great deal of hard work.

He sometimes wondered if Lambert really realized that when he spoke about wanting to enjoy more responsibility. He loved his son but in his heart he admitted Lambert was incapable of serious thought for long periods.

Especially when there were problems.

Like now.

A few minutes later a knock on the door heralded the entrance of his secretary. He held a file in his hand. 'Those papers you asked for, sir.'

'Ah good, thank you.'

'Will there be anything else?'

'Not for the moment.'

Once the man had gone, Hutchinson opened the file with hands that trembled slightly. Perhaps this would prove him wrong. He hoped so. What would he do otherwise? Unfortunately it didn't. The papers proved him oh-so-right. There was no mistake.

He sat back in his chair, taking off his reading glasses and rubbing his tired eyes. Damn, damn, damn! Someone was stealing money from the bank's accounts – a great deal of money too. But who was responsible or how long the thefts had been going on for, Hutchinson didn't know.

He meant to find out.

Three

'That was one of the best meals I've ever had.' Crowell leant back in his chair and smiled across at Mrs MacLean.

'Would you like some more?'

'No, thank you, ma'am, I couldn't possibly eat anything else.'

Norton and Hatcher nodded their agreement and Crowell knew there was no reason for them not to leave. But he remained where he was, reluctant to go. Wanting for a short while longer to enjoy again the pretence of a decent home and a family.

The sort of life he'd once had, but left behind for the excitement of becoming an outlaw. An excitement that had quickly died away in days of hard riding, poor food and sleeping on the ground in all kinds of weather. Even worse, in hurting people like the MacLeans. Making enemies of them.

He sighed. How could he go back now? He was a wanted man. He was headed for jail, or a shoot-out with a lawman.

'Is there anythin' we can do in return?'

'You can leave,' Veronica muttered.

17

Crowell took no notice. 'What about cutting more firewood?'

Mrs MacLean shook her head. 'No, we've got enough. Ronny, didn't you notice one of the corral rails coming loose? You could fix that. There's a hammer and nails in the barn.'

'OK, ma'am.'

'Are you sure?' Norton asked Crowell.

'Yeah, it'll be OK. It won't take long. You come with me. Hal, you stay here, help Mrs MacLean wash up.' And keep an eye on her was Crowell's unspoken message. The woman might appear sympathetic; that didn't mean she wouldn't shoot them given the chance to get her hands on the shotgun again. 'Miss Veronica, would you show us the rail?'

Without a word Veronica got up from the table and went outside with the two young men. As they started work she sat on the edge of the porch, back upright, hands twisted in her lap, watching them.

'I don't think she trusts us,' Norton said. 'Probably suspects we're gonna run off with the horses. We ain't, are we?'

It was a temptation. But horse stealing was a hanging offence and with the way their luck usually went, Crowell thought they'd be caught and strung up.

The afternoon sun was hot and there was no shade out by the corral. And it was hard work. Before long Mick and Bruce were dripping with sweat and they took off their vests and shirts. But at last the loose wooden pole was removed, a new one cut and sawed into the right shape and length and nailed into place.

Crowell decided they'd done a good enough job so

that even Veronica couldn't find fault with their work-manship. Wiping his neck with his bandanna, he went over to the water barrel near to where the girl sat and dipped his head into the cool water.

'So you've finished at last,' she said sarcastically. 'You sure took your time.'

'Oh, well, you know how it is with us desperadoes. We ain't used to hard work.' Crowell grinned.

For a moment it seemed as if Veronica might smile back, but just then Mrs MacLean and Hatcher came out of the house. Hal was carrying a couple of packages.

'Mick, Mrs MacLean has given us some coffee and tins of tomatoes and peaches.'

Veronica's face immediately turned mutinous again. 'For goodness sake, Ma, they've robbed us and eaten our dinner, now you're giving them our supplies!'

'They are down on their luck, dear.'

'So will we be soon!'

'Are you sure you can afford this?' Crowell asked.

'Ronny.' Mrs MacLean put a hand on the girl's arm in warning not to upset the men now they were ready to leave.

But Veronica took no notice, snapping out, 'Oh, take it like you've taken our money, and go! And don't pretend to be so damn grateful, you'd probably have stolen it anyway!'

'I'm sorry you feel so badly about us . . .'

'How the hell do you expect me to feel?'

'Perhaps you'd better go now,' Mrs MacLean said.

'Yes, ma'am, and you can forget all about us.'

Arm in arm Mrs MacLean and Veronica watched the three young men as they rode away. Both knew they had

had a lucky escape, that had the men been of a different kind to what they were, the encounter could have turned out badly for them.

'Oh, Ma,' Veronica said, tears coming into her eyes now that the danger was over.

'There, there it's all right, they're gone and we're safe. Nothing happened.' Mrs MacLean patted her daughter's arm. 'They were polite young men.'

'They robbed us!'

'But that was only because of their circumstances. It might be that all they need is a second chance in life to become worthwhile citizens.'

But Veronica wasn't prepared to be so forgiving. The safety of the ranch had been left in her hands. Although she knew what had happened wasn't her fault and that she couldn't have done anything to prevent it, she still felt she had let her father down and failed his trust.

'Perhaps a spell in jail is what they need! And if they ride into Cypress Grove and try to rob anyone there, I'm sure Marshal Franks will be more than a match for them and jail is where they'll end up. And a good job too!'

'What are we gonna do now?' Norton asked as they left the small ranch behind.

'Go on into Cypress Grove like we planned.'

They were hoping to find some place there to rob, or failing that get into a poker game, although with just two dollars and thirty-one cents between them Crowell wasn't very hopeful about that. They'd be laughed out of any decent game.

'Do you think we should?' Hatcher said. 'Supposing that gal takes it into her head to go into town and report us to the marshal?'

'She won't,' Crowell said with more conviction than he felt. 'But even if she does she won't want to leave her ma alone tonight. The earliest she'd set out will be tomorrow morning, so by the time she gets there we can be long gone.'

As they topped the hill, he paused to turn in the saddle and take a last look at the ranch.

'I wish we could afford to buy us a place like that.'

'Oh yeah, sure,' Norton said. 'With what exactly? We'd have to rob a bank or a train at least. More'n rob a general store anyhow.'

'Perhaps something'll turn up.'

Neither Norton nor Hatcher said any more. Clearly they didn't share Crowell's optimism.

Four

Cypress Grove was situated in a grassy meadow between two ranges of pine-clad hills, slopes rising gradually to snow-capped mountain peaks.

The town fathers knew what they were doing when they first chose this spot – not only was it beautiful, it was also surrounded by cattle country. Ranchers and their families needed stores in which to buy goods, cowboys needed saloons and dance-halls where they could let off steam; and because it was on the railroad line, cattle could be kept in pens to await shipment east or before being driven on to markets further west. It was a busy, ever-growing place, destined, its inhabitants hoped, for a successful future.

But when the train pulled in it was early evening, that time between the stores closing and the saloons getting into their stride. And the place appeared to be asleep. A few people got off the train along with Cobb and Neil, several others waited on the station platform, otherwise it was quiet.

With Neil carrying their carpet-bags, he and Cobb walked towards the road. They were almost there when

Cobb heard his name being called. Two men had emerged from the station office, derby hats in hands, smiles of greeting on their faces.

'Mr Cobb?' the elder of the two repeated.

'That's right.'

'Good. You've arrived safely. One hears so much talk of Indians and bandits one can never be sure of travel arrangements out here.'

'I don't think it's quite as bad as that. And you are?'

'Oh forgive me, dear chap, I'm sorry. I should have introduced myself. My name is Charles Quinn. I'm a Vice-President at the First Presidential Bank in New York. In charge of investments actually. And this is my personal assistant, Alec Beaumont.'

'Pleased to meet you, Mr Cobb.'

Quinn was in his fifties, Beaumont about thirty. Both had neat haircuts, thin moustaches and were dressed in eastern finery, with gold watch-chains stretched across their stomachs. They spoke with refined eastern accents.

'And are you going on this hunting trip too?' Cobb asked, with a slight frown. He hoped not. One greenhorn would be enough to cope with, three would be two too many.

Quinn laughed. 'Oh no, Mr Cobb, we have merely accompanied young Master Lambert to Cypress Grove to see no harm befell him on the journey. And we will naturally wait here for his return to escort him back to New York.'

Cobb wondered, but didn't like to ask, why a young man of twenty couldn't make the journey by himself. Perhaps it was because he was the son of a rich banker.

'We've booked you a room at the same hotel as Lambert,' Quinn went on. 'He's waiting to meet you there.'

'OK, let's go.' Cobb turned round to see Neil, about whom he'd forgotten, standing by his side, gaping at the two men as if hardly able to believe his eyes. 'By the way, this is Neil Travis. He's my, er, assistant.' And, not above showing off at times, Cobb felt quite pleased at how important that must sound to these easterners.

The town boasted a square lined with stores, a bank, a real estate office and on one corner the brick-built courthouse and marshal's office. There were two churches, a small school and a thriving business district. The sidewalks were clean, the buildings neat. And the saloons and dance-halls were situated out of the way, beyond the railroad tracks, so as not to disturb the respectable citizens, while not depriving the town's coffers of a cut from their revenue.

The Cypress Cattlemen's Hotel had shady porches, long windows, plush red curtains and carpets, crimson wallpaper and mahogany furniture.

Cobb was only thankful the cost of staying here, even for one night, wasn't coming out of Mr Bellington's coffers. Mr Bellington didn't like extravagant expense statements.

The clerk behind the reception desk looked down his nose at Cobb, who obviously did not come from the same class as the usual guests. But as the room was paid for he could do nothing but pass the visitors' book across to be signed; he seemed disappointed to find Cobb could write. He rang the bell for a porter.

Beaumont touched Cobb's arm. 'We didn't realize

you'd have anyone with you. I'm afraid we only booked one room.'

'And we're quite full up.' The clerk sounded delighted at being able to cause difficulties.

'That's OK, Neil can share with me. He can sleep on the floor.' Cobb wasn't particularly pleased at such an arrangement, but he felt it might be best to keep Neil, who was still gaping around at all the finery, where he could see him.

And Neil was only too agreeable, thinking the floor in such a hotel would be more comfortable than most of the beds in the sort of hotel he was used to. He would also be glad of Cobb's company, feeling ill-at-ease amongst both such well-off and unfamiliar men and all this splendour.

The clerk was about to object when an interruption came from upstairs.

Something heavy was flung to the floor and a petulant voice shouted, 'No! No! No! No! Gifford, how many bloody times must I tell you not those shoes with that suit? Bring me the ones with the tassels.'

'Tassels?' Neil asked, while Cobb looked at Quinn, eyebrows raised in query.

'Yes, sir,' Quinn confirmed Cobb's fears. 'That's Master Lambert.'

Oh God, Cobb thought miserably. 'Who's he shouting at?'

'Poor old Gifford,' Beaumont said with a little laugh, as if he was glad he wasn't the one on the receiving end of Lambert's temper. 'His valet.'

Neil said, 'What's a valet?'

Cobb didn't reply because he didn't know.

A few moments later Lambert Hutchinson ran down the stairs – so they were tassels, Neil thought, on his shoes? – all smiles, his tantrum forgotten.

'Mr Cobb! A pleasure to meet you at last!' Lambert put out a hand for Cobb to shake, which he did perhaps harder than necessary, for Lambert winced and gave a little uncomfortable laugh. All the same he went on enthusiastically, 'My uncle, Bellington, told me all about you when he decided you were to be my guide. I was most impressed. It seems you're quite a hero!'

'Yeah, well.' Cobb was embarrassed by the young man's eagerness.

Lambert's gaze fell on Neil but he immediately looked away, ignoring him. 'I trust my men have been looking after you?'

'Yes.'

'Good. Are we to start our trip tomorrow?' The tone said he hoped so.

Cobb nodded; the sooner they started the sooner this ordeal would be over.

'And there'll be plenty of game for me to shoot?'

'This time of the year, yeah.'

'Good-oh! Particularly buffalo. You must find me a big old buffalo to shoot. His shaggy head will look so fine adorning our dining-room wall.'

'Buffalo are pretty scarce these days.'

A look of the petulant temper that made him shout at his valet crossed Lambert's face, and in an icy tone he said, 'Oh, I think you'll do what I want, Mr Cobb.'

Or what? Cobb thought. He didn't like being threatened, especially by a greenhorn upstart, and it was with some difficulty he didn't lose his own temper.

26

Neil, who in their short acquaintance, had often been on the receiving end of Cobb's bad moods, grimaced.

'Mr Cobb will do his best,' Quinn said quickly, obviously recognizing what the darkening of Cobb's face meant in the same way that Neil did.

'Of course.' Lambert smiled again. 'Now I expect you'd like to freshen up and change into something suitable.'

'Suitable for what?'

'Why, a night on the town. You are to be my guest at dinner. I absolutely insist. And afterwards we'll go for a drink or two at a real saloon. I haven't yet had the chance to drink in a Western saloon and I simply must!'

'Good idea, what!' Quinn looked at Cobb, eyes begging him to agree.

'Jesus Christ!' Cobb exclaimed as soon as he and Neil were alone. 'How the hell am I going to put up with that goddamn brat?'

Cobb only swore if the occasion warranted it; which he decided this one surely did.

'Mr Cobb,' Neil turned from where he was admiring the bedroom and its furniture, 'am I included?'

'What, tonight?'

'Yeah.' Neil looked as if he hoped he would be left behind.

Cobb thought Lambert, and probably the other two as well, wouldn't expect Neil, who they all obviously regarded as some kind of servant like 'poor old Gifford', to be there, and wouldn't approve of his presence. But what the hell – Neil was with him and he wasn't going to leave the boy behind just because they were snobs.

'Yeah, of course.'

'I ain't got nothin' suitable to wear.' Certainly nothing with tassels on.

'Don't worry. Neither have I. This was meant to be a western hunting trip, not an eastern dinner party.'

Five

The Hutchinson party had a table in an alcove of the hotel dining-room. Crimson velvet drapes, crimson carpet. Silver cutlery and the best crockery. The best food the French chef could conjure up. Sparkling wines imported from the East.

And Cobb was right. Neil's presence was neither required nor expected. The table was laid for four and a fifth chair and fifth place had quickly to be found, which all three Easterners looked put out by.

And for his part, Neil wished he wasn't there. He felt very awkward, sure he would let Cobb down and show them both up. Used to just one knife and fork he wondered what all the cutlery was needed for. And used to plain eating he wondered what sort of food was being served up. Hoping he wouldn't do anything stupid, watching Cobb's every move, he sat, hunched over his plate, not saying a word, hardly eating, which for Neil, who was normally hungry, made a change.

Not that any one of them was really needed except as an audience for Lambert, who, even when eating and drinking, didn't stop talking.

Cobb thought his conversation could be divided into

29

chapters: 'My Life – Growing up with Papa and Mama; My Schooling; My Work in the Bank'.

Didn't the boy ever shut up? But it seemed not, for as if quite used to Lambert's boasting, Quinn and Beaumont sat looking at him with silly expressions, nodding or shaking their heads at appropriate intervals, but obviously just as bored with what Lambert said as Cobb was.

It was quite late by the time they'd finished and Cobb led the way to the red-light district. Lambert's eyes glittered with excitement at the activity.

In the darkness the saloons and dance-halls were lit up, gaudy and noisy, doing big business. The hitching rails were crowded with horses, and cowboys, townsmen and a few miners hurried along the sidewalks.

Some of the people stared, amused to see men in suits and shoes, but most were too busy to take much notice.

'Which saloon would you recommend we try, Mr Cobb?'

'What about that one?' Cobb chose it not because it was the biggest, the smallest, the most opulent or the cheapest, but simply because it was the nearest.

'The Deer's Horn, umm, yes, what a quaint name, I like it! Come along everyone.' Lambert plunged across the road and pushed open the batwing doors. 'I'm buying! What would you like?'

'He's generous, you've got to give him that,' Beaumont said in a whispered aside to Neil, careful not to let Quinn hear. 'Of course, it is all Daddy's money.'

Mr Bellington preferred that while on duty his detectives drank beer rather than anything stronger, but

Cobb felt in need of a double shot of rye. He frowned hard at Neil, forcing him to ask for a beer, and led the way over to a table in the corner where they could watch what was going on.

Light came from low-slung oil lamps. An enormous painting of an almost nude woman hung behind the bar. At a couple of tables some men were betting heavily on poker games, and a roulette wheel span in the opposite corner. A pianist belted out lively tunes on an old upright piano. Several girls wandered round the room, engaging men in conversation, before taking them through a door by the side of the bar, leading to the bedrooms.

'Good gracious! This is so exciting! The Real West!' Lambert exclaimed, staring at everything, his eyes alight with pleasure. 'I always imagined it would be something like this! So quaint! Everyone so easily pleased. And yet quite fascinating at the same time. Nothing like our New York inns, eh, Mr Quinn?' He downed his whiskey in one go.

'I should go easy on that if I were you, sir,' Quinn cautioned him. 'It's probably stronger than what you're used to.'

Lambert took no notice as he signalled to the bartender, asking for a bottle to be brought to their table. And it was soon clear that while Lambert was a braggart and a free spender, he wasn't able to hold his drink. He was already flushed from the wine he'd consumed at dinner, now he quickly became even redder-faced and extremely loud, causing several people at nearby tables to look and laugh.

While Quinn appeared uncomfortable and

Beaumont amused, Cobb wondered if he should stop Lambert from having any more whiskey. But he decided his duties didn't begin until they set out on the hunting trip. If Lambert couldn't handle his liquor he'd be the one to suffer from a hangover. Serve the pompous little idiot right!

'What about in here?' Crowell said as he, Norton and Hatcher stopped in front of The Deer's Horn Saloon. He pressed his nose against the window and peered inside. 'Don't look like nothin' we can't afford.'

The three young men had left their horses in the livery-stable, where it seemed only too likely they would also have to spend the night sleeping in the straw. They'd then headed for the red-light district, where they strolled up and down, taking in the sights, deciding where to go.

Crowell had quickly made up his mind that they couldn't rob anywhere in Cypress Grove. It had too much law. They'd already seen a tough-looking deputy walking along by the saloons, shotgun cradled in his arms, and an even tougher-looking marshal over by the railroad station. Instead, they just about had the time and money to enjoy a couple of beers, sleep in the stable and make a quick exit the following morning.

Having spotted the sign for 'Free Hard-boiled Eggs', both Norton and Hatcher agreed.

'Gosh Almighty! Look at her!' Lambert pointed to a girl with black hair, dark eyes and pink cheeks, and an extremely low-cut dress. 'What a beauty. I say, Mr Cobb, is she an Indian?'

'No,' Cobb said with a sigh.

'She looks like one to me. I wonder if I could buy her services. Then I could tell my friends I'd pleasured a wild squaw.'

'I shouldn't, sir.' Quinn looked quite horrified at the idea.

Lambert took as little notice of Quinn over a girl as over not drinking. He got unsteadily to his feet and, swaying a couple of times, went in pursuit of the black-haired prostitute.

'Oh dear,' Quinn said. 'Oh dear me.'

'Who the hell is this clown?' Hatcher said as he saw Lambert. 'Look at him! Whatever the hell has he got on?'

Lambert caught up with the girl by the bar. He stepped firmly in front of her, the manly effect spoiled as he then had to catch hold of the edge of the bar for support.

'Hallo, darling, what's your name?' he slurred.

'Angie.'

'That doesn't sound like an Indian's name. Here, lemme buy you a drink. Then I'll take you to bed.'

Normally Angie would have been only too delighted to accept both offers. She could sense quite easily when someone had money and with his well-cut clothes and air of elegance, this young man obviously had plenty. Unfortunately he was also drunk and Angie had had too much experience of drunks – rich and poor – to want to become involved with another one.

'No, thanks. And you've had quite enough to drink already.'

'Bartender, two whiskeys,' Lambert called, pounding the bar for emphasis. 'And be quick 'bout it.'

'I said no! And I ain't goin' upstairs with you. You'd do better to go back to wherever you came from and sleep it off.' Angie turned away.

No girl in Angie's position had ever said no to Lambert before.

'Don't you dare turn your back on me!' he shouted, and roughly caught hold of her arm, causing her to cry out, swinging her round. 'You're coming with me! How dare you bloody refuse me? Do you know who I am? You're just a whore and I want you! I intend to have you!'

'She said no.' Crowell stepped in between them. 'Out here when a lady says no, a gentleman accepts she means it. Let her go and go on about your business.'

'And you go to hell!' In a drunken fury, Lambert shoved Angie away from him and took a swing at Crowell.

Crowell stepped back, easily evading the blow, and let fly with his own fist. The punch caught Lambert half on the nose, half on the cheek, and felled him.

The boy landed on his back amongst the feet of the saloon's customers.

'Oh hell. Now what?' Cobb said, spotting the commotion over by the bar: men crowding round, voices raised in excitement.

'It's a fight,' Neil said.

'I can see that for myself.'

Was Lambert involved? As Cobb stood up he realized with a sinking feeling that Lambert was!

No wonder the boy had to be accompanied to

Cypress Grove; he was obviously the kind to get into trouble at the least provocation, and needed someone to look out for him.

A rangy-looking young man was about to launch himself forward to continue the fight when the black-haired whore screamed.

And someone else shouted, 'Look out! He's goin' for his gun!'

Six

'Oh *shit*!' Cobb exclaimed, with considerable feeling.

'Stop him, please!' Quinn begged. 'Hurry!'

Followed closely by the others, Cobb pushed his way through the crowd of men, who were trying to scramble out of the way of any stray bullets.

Lambert was fumbling with his gun, while Crowell had already drawn his.

'Stop! Don't shoot!'

Everyone stared at Cobb as he stepped between the two young men. At first Crowell didn't take any notice, shoving at Cobb to reach Lambert.

Cobb grabbed his arm, forcing the gun down until it was pointed at the floor.

'Let it be. He's drunk and stupid.'

'Mick, don't,' Norton added, pulling at his friend's arm. 'The kid ain't worth it.'

'Hell,' Crowell muttered. For a moment, Cobb didn't think he would take any notice, then, shrugging, he holstered his gun.

Cobb bent down, slapping Lambert's hand away from the gun he was still trying to drag from its holster. Catching hold of the boy's velvet collar, he hauled him to his feet.

'Lemme go!' Lambert yelled. He tried to struggle free, kicking out ineffectually at Cobb.

His back to Quinn so the man couldn't see him, Cobb hit Lambert hard round the back of his head.

'Ow! That hurt.'

'You're coming back to the hotel before you cause any more trouble. Now!' Zac glanced first at Angie then at Crowell and his two companions. 'Sorry.' Again Crowell shrugged. Holding none too gently on to Lambert's arm and neck, Cobb steered him towards the doors.

'Don't hurt him,' Quinn said, but otherwise made no attempt to interfere with the way his boss's son was being treated, while Beaumont was openly amused.

Cobb thought that what Lambert needed was a good thrashing, not treating gently, but, grim-faced, he said nothing.

'How dare you?' Lambert said as soon as they reached the sidewalk. 'Lemme go at once.'

Cobb pushed the boy away from him so he almost fell.

Following a nod from Quinn, Beaumont hurried over to the boy brushing him down until Lambert shouted, 'Stop that, you bloody fool! And, Cobb,' he pointed an unsteady finger at the man, 'you wait until Uncle Bell'ton hears how you treated me. I'll have you bloody sacked for this. You'll never work again.'

Wringing his hands together, Quinn said, 'Mr Cobb was only helping you. You could have been badly hurt.'

'I was handling the situ . . . situ . . . thing all right,' Lambert slurred his words, sounding haughty and drunk at the same time. 'That vulgar person, that

37

cowboy, dared hit me. Did you see? Me! He hit me! He deserved to be shot. I had the beating of him.'

'No you didn't. He'd have shot you. But if you had beaten him what then? Despite what you might believe, out here people aren't allowed to shoot dead those they consider beneath them. You'd have been arrested and charged with murder. Drunken stupidity wouldn't have been an excuse.'

'That's right.' Quinn took hold of Lambert's arm. 'Come along, sir, let's go back to the hotel and forget all about this, shall we?'

'Oh all right,' Lambert said sulkily and, turning away, made a funny noise and was promptly sick.

'Thanks for helping me,' Angie said, putting a hand on Crowell's arm. 'Can I do anything for you in return?' She considered the appearance of the young man and added, 'For free.'

'Mick,' Norton warned. 'We oughtta go.'

'Why?' Crowell said angrily. He hadn't had a woman in some time and Angie was young and extremely pretty, not the sort he could often afford, and here she was offering herself to him for nothing.

'Because that damn kid and his friends might report what happened to the marshal. And then who d'you think is gonna be in trouble? Not them. Us.'

Crowell sighed impatiently. Unfortunately Bruce was right. He didn't think the incident was serious enough to involve the law, but the strangers might believe otherwise. And the marshal would soon recognize them as wanted outlaws and they'd be the ones to land up in jail. It wasn't fair.

'Sorry, darlin'. My friend's right. We've gotta be goin'.'

Angie pulled a face. 'That's a shame.'

'Sure is,' Hatcher agreed. 'We ain't even had any free eggs yet.'

Somehow Lambert, supported by Quinn and Beaumont, was escorted back to the hotel without further incident. As they reached the door to his room, it opened and a worried-looking Gifford, who was a pale, plump man, hurried out.

'Oh dear, sir, what's happened?' He spoke with an English accent.

'Gifford, I don't feel well,' Lambert said piteously. 'Put me to bed will you? Make everything stop swinging round.'

'See he's cleaned up.'

'Certainly, Mr Quinn. You can leave him in my hands.'

'Jesus,' Cobb muttered. 'We're leaving early in the morning. Real early. Will he be able to make it?'

'I'll see he's ready, sir.'

Once the bedroom door closed, Quinn ran a hand over tired eyes and said, 'I'm sorry about this, Mr Cobb. Lambert is only young and sometimes his high spirits make him act a little wildly.'

'Yeah, well, out here acting a little wildly can get you killed, however young and high-spirited you are. And out here by the time a man reaches twenty he's considered grown.'

Quinn flushed. 'I appreciate that. I'm sure it won't happen again. Lambert is a little spoiled . . .'

'Spoiled rotten actually,' Beaumont said in Neil's ear.
'. . . but he is on the whole good natured. By morning he'll have forgotten his threats and merely be looking forward to his hunting trip. I assure you he won't report you to Mr Bellington. Mr Cobb?'

'Yeah?'

'Those young men in the saloon, they won't cause any more trouble will they?'

'I doubt it. Nothing I can't handle anyhow. But I've a feeling they're wanted by the law and will keep out of the way in case the marshal gets to hear about the fight.'

'Good heavens,' Beaumont said, surprised. 'Really? How do you know that?'

'They had the look of unsuccessful outlaws to me. Be around thieves long enough, you soon recognize the type.' And Cobb glared at Neil.

'Oh well, so long as you think everything will be all right,' Quinn said. 'Goodnight, Mr Cobb, er . . . Travis. We'll see you in the morning.'

'Yeah, early.'

Not exactly in a good mood, Cobb stalked along the corridor to his own room. Once there he took a pillow off the bed and threw it at Neil. 'Like I said you can sleep on the floor. Use a couple of coats for blankets.'

Neil was cross. It seemed most unfair that Cobb was taking his ill temper out on him, but he didn't risk saying anything. Whenever he'd objected to what Gary, his elder brother, did, Gary had beaten him up; Cobb might just do the same.

'I'll stay behind if that'll make it easier for you,' he offered, thinking it might be easier for him as well.

Cobb stared at the boy in surprise. 'What are you talking about?'

'It's obvious Lambert, er, Mr Hutchinson, doesn't like or approve of me. Perhaps he'd behave better if I wasn't around.'

'I doubt that. That silly brat doesn't know what behaving well means. And, Neil, if I've got to suffer the silly brat's company, so have you!'

An hour later, when the streets were silent and for the most part empty, except for a few stragglers returning home from the saloons, one of the hotel's bedroom doors opened. A figure slipped out into the hall, paused to make sure he was alone and unheard, then tiptoed down the back staircase.

The man let himself out of the kitchen door, jamming it open so he would be able to get back in. Sticking to the shadows, he made his way down to the livery-stable.

He wondered where the three men – the outlaws – who'd tangled with Lambert had gone. It didn't matter. He had all night to find them.

'Let's camp here,' Crowell said as they came to a clearing in the pine-trees.

'We ain't that far away from town,' Hatcher pointed out. 'Supposing someone comes after us?'

'They won't now. It's too late and too dark. We'll just have to make sure we're on our way at first light.'

All three were tired and fed up. Instead of being in the comparative comfort of Cypress Grove's livery-stable, having enjoyed a couple of drinks and free eggs, they were riding deeper into unknown woods, with no real idea of where they were going or what sort of future lay ahead of them.

'Perhaps,' Crowell said hopefully, trying to keep up his friends' spirits, as a good leader should, 'things'll look better in the morning.' The trouble was he didn't believe it himself.

Unable to sleep, Mick lay awake for a long while as the little camp fell quiet, except for Norton's snoring and the snuffling of the horses. The fire had burnt down almost to its embers and, feeling cold, he turned over, pulling the blanket up under his chin. At the same time he heard the sound of a horse crashing through the undergrowth, coming closer.

'What the hell!' Heart beating rapidly, he sat up straight, hand reaching for his gun. Maybe he'd been wrong and the marshal had already started out after them. 'Wake up! Quick!'

'What's the matter?' Norton asked sleepily, while Hatcher raised himself up on his elbows.

'We've got company.' Crowell got to his feet.

'No need for that, gentlemen.' A rider had emerged from the trees. 'You can put your guns away. I'm unarmed and I mean you no harm.'

But, Crowell thought, the rider meant harm to someone. He was muffled up in a dark cloak, a hat pulled low over his forehead while a bandanna covered the rest of his face, making it impossible to see what he looked like.

'What d'you want?' Norton asked, coming to stand by Crowell's side.

'Would I be right in saying that the three of you are

42

wanted by the law?'

'Who told you that?' Crowell demanded belligerently.

'So you are outlaws. But from the look of you you're not very successful. Perhaps I can help you out.'

'What do you mean?'

'Do exactly as I tell you and you'll be well rewarded. Ah, you don't look convinced. At least hear me out. What have you to lose?'

Seven

Despite their late night, Cobb and Neil were up and ready for the hotel's first serving of breakfast. Looking pale and weary, Quinn joined them.

'Where is he?' Cobb asked grumpily, staring pointedly at the dining-room clock. It was half past seven.

'It is early.'

'That's right. I said we were leaving early.'

'I'm afraid Lambert never gets up much before ten o'clock. Especially if he's had a late night. No one expects anything different. And we were up very late.'

'And he was drunk,' Cobb added angrily.

'I know. I'm sorry. I feel this is partly my fault.'

Cobb didn't contradict the man. 'I've a good mind to go up there and haul his damn ass out of bed.'

'Oh no, please don't do that!' Quinn exclaimed, looking shocked at both the idea and the language. 'I realize Lambert and his ways are different to what you're used to, and he's not always considerate of others. But please at least try to understand it's not necessarily his fault. No one has ever told him no. He's always been allowed to get away with anything he does and have whatever he wants. He really isn't a bad boy at heart.'

Cobb didn't exactly see things the same way.

'I'll make sure Lambert is down as soon as possible.'

'See you do.' Zac threw his napkin down on the table and stood up. 'Come on, Neil, let's go. We'll be at the livery-stable.'

Now, several hours later, Neil sat on an upturned barrel, not daring to say a word, while a grim-faced Cobb paced about in the stable doorway, pausing now and then to look along the street.

The horses were saddled and bridled, the packhorse loaded with supplies. Everything was ready. Except that of Lambert Hutchinson there was still no sign.

If, Neil thought, the rest of the trip was going to be like this, it would be dreadful. But he had the feeling that once away from Cypress Grove and the presence of Quinn and Beaumont, Cobb would lay down a few rules for Master Lambert, which the boy would either keep or break at his peril.

Despite no one having reported the fight in The Deer Horn Saloon – it hardly being worthy of being called a fight, let alone being reported – Marshal Franks had heard about it nonetheless.

Ted Franks was a good lawman. Hard when he had to be, capable and an accurate shot. He'd been marshal of Cypress Grove for a number of years. He liked the town, and as the citizens expressed satisfaction with the way he did his job, he expected to end his working life there.

He also enjoyed a good relationship with the town council, who recognized the many advantages expert law brought with it. They were generous enough that

Franks could afford to hire able men as his deputies.

Drew Patterson was the latest in a long line of young men willing to wear a badge. He was in his late teens, and tough, if perhaps still a little green.

'There were three of 'em,' Drew said, pouring out coffee for himself and the marshal. 'In their early twenties. According to Angie what happened was the fault of that posh kid been staying at the hotel. He started it.'

Franks sighed, not surprised. The kid hadn't been in town long, but had spent that time strutting around as if both the place and the people were beneath him.

'And the men with the kid were the ones stopped it before it got out of hand. They went back to the hotel and the other three left the saloon. After I spoke to Angie, I went down to the livery but they hadn't wasted any time and had already skedaddled.'

'Umm . . . I wonder why if the fight wasn't all that serious.'

'Mebbe they were scared of becoming involved with the law.'

'Just what I was thinking. Perhaps you could take some of the wanted posters down to Angie, see if she recognizes the three men on any of 'em. And in the meantime, Drew, keep your eyes open.'

'You think they'll be back?'

'Mebbe.' Franks took a drink of the coffee and added, 'Still, they don't sound like the most dangerous outlaws we'll ever come across, and I doubt if we'll hear anything from 'em again.

'Mr Cobb,' Neil called from the stable doorway. 'Lambert is here. Come and see.'

Strolling unhurriedly down the street, Lambert was accompanied by Quinn and Beaumont. Behind them struggled Gifford, who was carrying what looked like a great deal of luggage.

Lambert was dressed up in what he obviously considered the most splendid western finery: Stetson hat, decorated with several eagle feathers, fringed buckskin shirt and matching trousers, hand-tooled leather boots, and a leather belt and double holster in which rested two silver-plated Colt .45s.

Cobb and Neil looked at one another and, horrified, Cobb exclaimed, 'Good God! He looks like someone out of a fancy circus!'

Neil hurriedly retreated to the far side of the horses where he buried his face in his animal's neck and gave way to a fit of helpless laughter; both at Lambert's ludicrous outfit and at Cobb's horror.

Made of sterner stuff, Cobb stood waiting in the doorway.

'Good morning, Mr Cobb,' Lambert called out happily. 'I hope I haven't kept you waiting long. Lovely weather to start out, what? Do you like my suit, I bought it specially, just the thing for the frontier, don't you agree?'

'Yes, very nice.'

The stable-owner grinned and whispered, 'Who the hell is that? I ain't never seen anyone quite like him before!'

And Neil collapsed in a fresh fit of laughter.

'Er . . . what's all that?' Cobb nodded at the cases Gifford placed carefully on the ground.

'The clothes and equipment I'll need on the trail.'

Lambert sounded very surprised at the question. 'There's no need for you to concern yourself with it, Mr Cobb, Gifford will look after everything for me, as he always does, won't you, Gifford?'

'Yes, certainly, sir.'

'You mean Gifford is coming with us?'

'But of course. I thought you understood that.' Lambert frowned. 'Mr Cobb, I see you've provided only one packhorse. We shall, of course, need another one. See to it at once, will you? And we need a horse for Gifford to ride. A nice gentle one because Gifford doesn't like and isn't used to horses.'

'Then wouldn't it be best if he was left behind?'

Lambert looked quite shocked. 'I can't possibly go anywhere without my valet to help me wash and dress.'

'Oh, right.'

'No, no! We shall just have to accommodate him by riding slowly at first and waiting for him when he falls off, damn nuisance, what? Now how about that brown mare?' Spotting Neil, Lambert added imperiously, 'You boy, saddle the mare. And help Gifford load my luggage on a packhorse. Hurry it up, there's a good chap.'

Cobb went over to Neil. 'Do what the silly sonofabitch wants. And if you keep laughing I'll have your hide.'

'I'm sorry, I can't help it.' Neil tried to control himself, but with another snort had to turn away.

Watched by the stable-owner, as well as a curious gathering of noisy, pointing urchins – none of which improved Cobb's temper – everything was finally sorted out. While Cobb might be red in the face, ready to explode at any moment, Lambert, excited and eager, seemed oblivious to the stir he was creating. Or maybe he was pleased about it, thinking it was because everyone was impressed by him, rather than entertained.

'Best get started, what?' he said, leaping up into the saddle.

'Here, let me help you,' Neil said to Gifford, who was struggling to mount his horse.

'Thank you, sir.' The man's pale face was even paler, and he was shaking slightly. 'I cannot say I am looking forward to this ride.'

'Then why are you goin'?'

'It's my duty, sir.'

'Goodbye, Quinn, Beaumont, we'll see you in a couple of weeks' time.'

'Goodbye, sir, have a good trip.'

'Oh I shall I'm sure.'

Did a collective sigh of relief at their final departure go up from the two men left behind? Cobb thought so. But his own sigh was one of despair, because now he had Lambert Hutchinson, spoiled, arrogant, stupid, to himself; along with an English valet, who couldn't ride and was quite unsuitably dressed in a black suit, white shirt and shoes, but who was necessary because Lambert still couldn't dress himself.

He just hoped none of the other detectives employed by Bellington's ever found out about this indignity!

Eight

Cobb led the way down the stagecoach road out of town. Before long they turned off on to a track that led towards the pine-clad foothills. Mid-afternoon found them crossing a meadow known locally as Tyler's Rocks, named after the large outcrop of rocks and boulders that lay in its centre. Beyond was wilderness and the first slopes of the mountains.

From a safe distance behind, Crowell, Norton and Hatcher followed.

'Ain't they goin' slow?' Norton said.

'That's because of . . . oops, there he goes again!' Crowell grinned as they watched Gifford fall from the back of his horse. Everything came to a halt while he was helped on again.

Even from here they could recognize the frustration of the man, Cobb.

'Be so easy it'll be like taking pot-shots at rabbits,' Norton mumbled.

'I ain't sure I like it,' Hatcher objected. 'It don't seem right to me.'

No one spoke. For what they'd agreed to do didn't seem right to any of them.

'It ain't too late to back out.'

Crowell said, 'But, Hal, the muffled man's goin' to pay us two thousand dollars.'

Two thousand dollars! More than any of them had ever seen; ever imagined.

'It still don't make it right.'

'I know but just think what we can do with that much money. Why, we can go down into Colorado, where we ain't wanted, and buy some land, start our own place.' Which was something they all dreamt about.

'Wonder who that gent was?' Hatcher said, still trying to raise objections.

'Does it matter?'

'I mean, can we trust him when we don't know who he is? Why wouldn't he show us his face?'

'He gave us money to be goin' on with, didn't he?' Crowell jingled some coins in his pocket. 'I reckon he's good for the rest of it. What d'you think, Bruce?'

'Yeah, I guess,' Norton nodded reluctantly.

'Look, I don't really wanna do somethin' like this but if we don't we've got nothin'. We've reached rock-bottom.' Crowell felt no happier than Hal about the stranger's early morning visit to their camp and the scheme he'd put to them. But he could see no risks. 'And this'll be easy money. How can we have any trouble?'

Norton and Hatcher glanced at one another. Mick often said that sort of thing. His plans rarely worked out quite so well. Unfortunately he was right about one thing: they were down to their last few dimes, and the only alternatives to starving were committing another small-time robbery, in an area where they were already wanted and where the law was tough and good; getting a job; or doing what the stranger wanted.

And two thousand dollars – it was surely too good an opportunity to miss out on. And, surely, there wouldn't be any danger.

Against their better judgment, not wanting to sound afraid, wanting to act like the desperadoes they fooled themselves into believing they were, all three allowed themselves to be persuaded.

'How do we go about it?' Norton asked.

'We follow 'em. Pick our moment and act fast! I reckon the only one we've gotta worry about is Cobb, but he shouldn't present any real problem to the three of us.'

Before it started to get dark, Cobb found a suitable place to stop for the night: a clearing amongst the dense undergrowth, sheltered by trees and rocks, over-looking a river far below.

'A most splendid place to stop, what!' Lambert exclaimed. He dismounted and flung the reins of his horse at Gifford.

'No, see to your own animal,' Cobb told him.

'My God, sir! I never do manual work of any kind.'

'Gifford is tired, sunburnt and hurt from all those falls he took. He needs to rest. In fact you can look after his animal as well.'

'It's all right, sir,' Gifford protested. 'I'll do it.'

'No, you won't. You go over there and sit down.'

'What about your boy?' Lambert said with a nod at

Neil. 'I thought he was your servant and was along to do all the dirty work.'

'Then you thought wrong. Neil has his own horse to see to, and afterwards he's got to gather up some wood for a fire, because it'll be cold once the sun goes down. Just do as you're told. You wanted to come along on a western trip and the first thing a westerner learns is to look after his own horse.'

It took Lambert a long time of fumbling about to unsaddle the two horses, for it was a task he'd never had to perform before. He didn't know whether or not to sulk about it or find it interesting. Nor did he know whether to be cross about Cobb's attitude. Cobb was in danger of getting above himself, but at the same time Lambert did want to behave as if he was a real westerner, even if it meant doing things he considered beneath him.

When he'd finished he sat down in front of the fire Neil had started and, immediately forgetting all about his sulk, said, 'Mr Cobb, now we're out on the trail, and having noted westerners' somewhat unfortunate informality even with strangers, I've decided to give you permission to call me Lambert. I presume I may call you Zac?'

'Yeah, I suppose so.'

Neil noticed that Lambert's informality didn't extend to offering him the chance to call him anything except Mr Hutchinson.

'And what do we call you?' Cobb said, going over and bending down by the valet, who looked quite old.

'Why, Gifford, sir.'

'No, your Christian name. And there's no need for

53

all this sir business. Certainly not with Neil and not with me either. You can call me Zac.'

'Oh no, sir, I couldn't possibly! It wouldn't be right, not at all.'

'Well, I can't keep on calling you Gifford. I wouldn't find that right. So what's your name?'

'It's . . .' – the man paused as if he hadn't used his Christian name in such a long time he'd forgotten what it was – '. . . George. But I'd really much prefer if you called me Gifford, sir. It's what I'm used to.'

Cobb put a hand on the man's shoulder. 'Don't worry.'

'Zac,' Lambert called, 'where do we sleep? I don't see any tents or beds.'

'I can't stand it,' Cobb muttered, making Neil want to laugh both at the suggestion and at Cobb's reaction. 'What does the silly fool expect? A hotel?' He turned to Lambert. 'We sleep on the ground out in the open.'

'Oh . . . but . . . how awful! Out here?'

'That's right.'

'Might there not be wild animals about?'

'The fire will keep them away. We'll be safe enough.'

Lambert didn't look too sure about that, nor quite as happy about this trip as when they'd started out. So far nothing had worked out as he had imagined, which had included him wallowing in luxury as he usually did. But like all his moods and tempers, his apprehension was soon forgotten.

'What's for supper? I'm starving. Gifford, didn't you pack some tins of quails' eggs? We'll have them tonight. And some champagne.'

'Yes, sir, I'll get them and cook them for you.'

'No you won't.' Cobb pushed the man down. 'We'll all have bacon and beans.'

'Bacon and beans! What sort of food is that?' Lambert objected, looking most displeased. 'I can't eat that.'

'Yeah you can and will. A westerner doesn't eat quails' eggs, whatever they are. He has bacon and beans and coffee strong enough to stand his spoon up in!'

Nine

'Gifford, my gun. No, not that one, you bloody fool. My new Winchester. I need a rifle with which to shoot rabbits. Don't you know anything?'

'I'm sorry, sir.'

Cobb gritted his teeth together. He didn't know at whom to feel angriest: Lambert for his constant rudeness to his valet, or Gifford for apologizing for things that weren't his fault.

'It's my job,' Gifford had tried to explain on more than one occasion when Cobb said he didn't understand how the man put up with Lambert's behaviour. 'I don't mind. And on the whole Master Lambert is a thoughtful employer.'

Cobb hadn't seen much evidence of that. And he'd quickly decided that if ever Lambert dared speak so rudely to him he was going to paddle the boy's behind for him. So far, Lambert hadn't been openly rude to him, but whether that was because he feared or respected the private detective, Cobb didn't know.

Now Lambert dismounted and threw the reins of his horse towards Neil. 'You, boy, hold my horse.'

'OK,' Neil said mutinously. He was as fed up with

Lambert as Cobb. Fed up with his 'You, boy, do this, do that' with never a 'please' or 'thank you'. Despite his upbringing, being abused by father and older brother, and his life on the road as a thief, Neil was on the whole good-natured, but even he had his limits.

Seemingly unaware of the feelings of his guides, Lambert took hold of the rifle and walked forward a little way. He raised the weapon to his shoulder, aimed, fired and shot yet another rabbit, crying out in delight.

Not that he wanted it, either to eat or as a trophy. He probably wouldn't even go and pick it up, or rather send Gifford to pick it up for him. The only trophy he was interested in taking home was a buffalo's head and the rabbit, like everything else he'd shot, would be left where it fell.

They were three days into the trip and deep within the foothills, the mountain slopes looming close by. The trees grew thickly all round them – pine mostly, but also larch and aspen – the undergrowth almost impenetrable at times, but now and then they came to an upland meadow where grass waved knee-high, colourful flowers growing in the shade at the edges.

They had found plenty of animals – rabbits, deer, elk – all of which had fallen to Lambert's fancy guns, for he was a good shot, hitting whatever he aimed at. Once Cobb recognized bear sign, but he'd said nothing. He had no desire to see a bear killed needlessly, nor for a bear to attack Lambert, who, as well as being a good shot, was also a reckless one, getting as close to his quarry as he possibly could.

But there were no buffalo. Once great herds had

roamed the area, but most had fallen to the guns of earlier hunters.

All morning they had ridden by the winding, sandy banks of a deep, rushing river. Cobb thought if any of the few buffalo still left were about, they would come to the water to drink. So far he'd seen no sign of any. He was getting almost as anxious as Lambert, for he was sure the boy wouldn't agree to return to Cypress Grove until he'd bagged the animal he'd set his heart on shooting.

Lambert was also an expert horseman, fearless at tackling whatever they came across. Unfortunately he wasn't so good at obeying orders or pulling his weight.

Roundabout noon, Cobb decided they should stop for a couple of hours to rest the horses. Before Lambert could be told to do anything, Gifford bustled around, doing everything for him. As usual, Lambert allowed him to get on with it. He relaxed on the ground, looking forward to eating some of the quails' eggs of which he was so fond.

'Ah, this is the life, what! Warm sun, cool breeze, the sound of a river. What a wonderful country! Good company. Good food. Hurry up, Gifford, I'm hungry.'

Cobb glanced across at Gifford. The man still hadn't mastered the art of horse riding. He was moving stiffly, seeming to be in pain. And there was Lambert, young and fit, lazing about, shouting out his orders to the man. It rarely took much for Cobb to lose his temper. It was a wonder he hadn't lost it already. He lost it now.

'It would be even better if you helped Gifford.'

'He's paid to do the work. It's what I employ him for.'

'You seem to think the answer to all life's problems lies in money.'

58

'Doesn't it?'

'Not always, which maybe you'd realize if you got off your ass and did something for a change.'

'Mr Cobb, please,' Gifford said, wringing his hands together.

'There's no need to be so rude.' Lambert was clearly shocked both at Cobb's tone and his sentiments.

He wasn't used to people shouting at him. Back in New York no one he came into contact with ever dared be rude to him; mostly for fear of upsetting his rich father. And he had ways and means of dealing with anyone who did, in some way, upset him, which he didn't hesitate to use. So now he didn't intend to let someone like Cobb, uneducated and a westerner, get away with such behaviour.

'You know, if this trip goes well I intend to speak on your behalf to Uncle Bellington. But so far I think I have cause for dissatisfaction.'

'Oh?' said Cobb ominously, while Neil looked on appalled sure Lambert had gone too far and Cobb was about to explode.

'Yes. You have failed in finding any buffalo for me to shoot. I seem to remember specifically telling you I wanted a buffalo's head as a trophy.'

'I can't find what's not there. I warned you we might not have any luck.'

Lambert took no notice. He nodded in Neil's direction. 'And I really don't know why you've brought that person along. What exactly is he here for? He doesn't do anything.'

'Neil is my helper.'

'Well, I think he's a disgrace.'

'I don't care what you think.'

'Mr Cobb, please remember you're in my employ and should take notice of what I say and what I want. I wouldn't like to have to tell Uncle Bellington you'd failed me.'

'Why you little spoilt. . . !' Cobb stepped forward.

Lambert, alarmed at the look on the man's face, hastily scrambled to his feet. Perhaps, after all, he hadn't been wise in trying to assert his authority. Who knew what these westerners, brought up with violence and with little appreciation for the finer things in life, were capable of?

'Please, sir, no!' Gifford cried. Hastily he got between Cobb and Lambert. 'He doesn't mean it. Please, sir.'

Red in the face, Cobb slowly unclenched his fists. He couldn't stay here any longer. He had to get away or do something he might regret. 'Neil, come with me.'

'Where are we goin'?' Neil asked.

'Where are you going?' Lambert asked, a note of panic in his voice as if he feared Cobb might be about to leave him and Gifford alone in the wilderness.

Cobb shouted, 'To look for the goddamn buffalo you're so anxious to shoot!'

Lambert relaxed immediately, face suddenly wreathed in smiles. 'Oh! Good idea, what! Don't be long will you? Oh, Gifford, another glass of champagne.'

Cobb muttered something, which luckily no one else heard.

As they rode away amongst the trees, Neil also risked being yelled at and said, 'D'you think we'll find any buffalo?'

'No. I just had to get away from that silly sonofabitch and I didn't want him bullying you while I wasn't there.'

Neil, who didn't think Cobb cared about him or his feelings one way or the other, found himself pleased about that. 'What will you do if he tells Mr Bellington you deliberately failed him?'

'I hope Mr Bellington will understand I did my best. If not, there's not much I can do.' Cobb shrugged but he was deeply angry at the thought of losing the job he loved because of the spoilt, ill-mannered and extremely foolish Lambert Hutchinson. 'Way things are going, he won't get back to Cypress Grove to tell Mr Bellington anything. I'll drown the bastard first!'

The Crowell gang had ridden as near as they dared to the hunting party, watching out for their chance. So far it hadn't come. The four riders kept together and, while none of them admitted it out loud, they didn't like the idea of going up against Cobb, a man who looked as if he wouldn't be afraid to pull his gun and when he did so would know how to use it.

They were becoming anxious, wanting to get this over and done with, thinking that the longer they had to follow on behind, the greater the possibility of being spotted.

They were taking it in turns for two of them to hang back, hidden amongst the trees, while the third stayed within sight of their quarry.

Crowell and Norton were sitting on the ground, getting their own noon-day meal ready when Hatcher rode up. He looked excited and scared all at the same time.

'Mick! Bruce! Cobb and the kid have ridden out. The old man and the boy are on their own.'

'Good.' Crowell stood up feeling pleased, even if his heart started to beat wildly. Now there could be no excuse not to act. 'Let's go. Get it over with.'

Ten

'I do hope Mr Cobb has some luck.' Lambert handed his glass to Gifford for him to refill. 'Well, he'd better.'

'Yes, sir. Maybe though he's right when he says there aren't any buffalo to be found.'

Lambert sighed in exasperation. 'Of course there are buffalo! I want to shoot one. I intend to shoot one and nothing anyone says is going to stop—'

'What's that, sir?'

'What's what?' Lambert demanded crossly, not liking an interruption when he was in full complaining flow.

Before Gifford had a chance to answer, three riders, guns in their hands, galloped out of the trees. And raced towards them.

'Sir!' Gifford cried out in horror.

When he sat down, Lambert had taken off his leather holster with its two fancy guns, placing it carefully by his coat, where he could admire it. Heart pounding, he dived for the holster. He didn't reach it as Crowell rode between him and it.

'Don't try anythin'!'

'Master Lambert!' In a panic, Gifford ran towards Lambert. Straight into Norton's horse. Norton had no chance to avoid him and the old man was knocked off his feet to land in a crumpled, unmoving heap.

'Hell!' Crowell swore. No one was meant to be hurt. He dragged his own horse around, getting ready to dismount.

And Lambert seized the chance to leap to his feet and take off at a run. He had no idea where to go. How to escape. No idea of what the men wanted. Except that, whatever it was, it boded ill for him.

'Zac, help! Someone! Help me!' he screamed uselessly. And angrily, thinking that Cobb was nowhere nearby now when he was needed.

Nodding at the valet, Crowell said to Hatcher, 'See to him if you can.'

He urged his horse into a gallop after Lambert, catching up with him at the river's edge. With a look of terror on his face, Lambert dodged this way and that, attempting to keep out of the horse's way. Crowell eased himself out of the saddle and, with a wild yell, leapt at the boy, catching him round the waist.

Together they slid uncontrollably on the wet sandbank and, arms round each other, tumbled over the edge into the water. It was deep, cold and fast-running, sweeping them off their feet, threatening to carry them downstream.

Crowell recovered first. He was a strong swimmer and he kicked to the surface, gasping for breath, shivering. He reached out, somehow managing to grab hold of Lambert's collar as the boy swept by him. Lambert came up, spluttering and coughing, arms and legs flailing in panic.

'Stop it!' Crowell yelled. 'I've got you.'

But Lambert couldn't swim and, sure he was about to drown, struggled violently. Crowell lost his footing and went under again, almost losing his grasp on the boy.

By now Norton had ridden up. Quickly he threw a rope at Crowell. 'Mick, catch it!'

At his second attempt, Mick got hold of the rope. With his free hand he tied it round his waist. 'OK, pull!'

Norton urged his horse backwards and Crowell swam for the shore, dragging Lambert after him.

As soon as they could stand, the water rushing by their knees, Lambert wrestled free and aimed a punch at Crowell. He had no better luck now than in the saloon. Crowell ducked out of the way, the feeble blow catching him on the shoulder. He shoved the boy aside and Lambert slipped, sitting down. Crowell moved swiftly, grabbing Lambert's shoulders, turning him round and holding his head under the water.

'Mick,' Norton warned. 'Don't kill him.'

Crowell let Lambert go and the boy came up choking, coughing up water.

Normally Crowell wouldn't have treated anyone so violently. But this was not going in the quick, smooth way he'd planned and hoped for. He was scared Cobb and the kid would ride back any moment and start shooting; spoil everything. He wanted to get away fast and easy, and for that he needed Lambert not only to be their captive but a compliant one too.

So he growled in the boy's ear, 'I can keep doin' that and I will, if'n you give me any more goddamn trouble. So get on up there and shut up.'

Lambert was shoved towards the bank where Norton grabbed his arms, pulling him up and out of the river.

While Crowell stood nearby, bent forward, hands on his knees, breathing heavily, Lambert collapsed on the ground, feeling sick.

Once he had regained his breath he looked up at the two men and moaned most piteously, 'What do you want? Please don't kill me. I've got money. I'll give you whatever you want. Oh, please, please spare me.'

Crowell kicked his legs, but not hard. 'You're comin' with us.'

'Why?'

Neither man answered.

'We'd better get outta here in case those other two ain't long.' Norton looked over his shoulder as if expecting to see Cobb and Neil emerging from the trees.

Crowell nodded in agreement. With Norton leading the two horses, he manhandled Lambert back to where Hatcher waited. Hal was bent over Gifford and now he stood up, shrugging. The valet lay where he had fallen, pale-faced, eyes closed.

'Gifford, get up at once, help me,' Lambert whined.

'Hell!' Norton said in disgust. 'He's hurt, can't you see that?' He turned to Crowell. 'I didn't mean to hurt him. He came at me out of nowhere. What shall we do with him?'

'We can't do nothin'. We'll have to leave him here,' Crowell decided. 'He'll be better off with Cobb. Cover him with a blanket, make him as comfortable as possible. Where's the rope?'

'What do you think you're doing?' Lambert demanded in a hysterical tone.

'Tying you up.'

'You can't do that! How dare you? Let me go at once. Do you know who I am?'

'Yeah.'

'You do?' Lambert was most surprised.

'Yeah. You're Lambert Hutchinson from New York.'

'How do you know that? Who told you? Why are you doing this?'

Taking no notice of all these questions, Crowell swung the boy round and, forcing his arms behind him, tied the rope round his wrists.

'Ow! Don't. Oh, that's too tight. It hurts.'

'Make it easy on yourself and stop moaning,' Norton advised.

Naturally Lambert, who rarely listened to anyone's advice and certainly not that of those he considered beneath him, took no notice. 'I demand you stop this at once. Do you hear me? My father will never let you get away with this.'

Crowell lost all patience. 'Shut up!' he yelled. He drew his bandanna from round his neck and shoved it into Lambert's mouth, tying it tight.

'Are you OK?' Norton asked him.

'What d'you mean?'

'You and the kid are both wet through.'

'Can't do nothin' about that right now.'

'Shouldn't you get dry?'

'There ain't time. It ain't cold. We'll get dry when we can. Get him up on the horse.'

Lambert found his uncomfortable ordeal far from over. To his horror he was picked up and pushed, belly-down, over the back of his horse. He wanted to protest but he couldn't with the wet and dirty bandanna stuffed in his mouth. He was tied to the saddle and in this extremely awkward manner he was led, bouncing and jolting, back towards the river.

As the horses splashed into the water, Crowell looked at Norton and Hatcher. He grinned and punched his arm in the air. They'd done it. Got away with it. All without firing a single shot. Of course, it was a shame about that old guy. But that had been an accident and Crowell hoped he wasn't too badly hurt.

Now all they had to do was ride to the line shack they'd passed on their way into Cypress Grove. And there wait for the muffled man. And his two thousand dollars.

Lambert was naturally not nearly so happy. In fact, he was terrified, near to tears. He couldn't believe this was happening to him. Didn't understand what was happening. Where had these men come from? What did they want with him? They knew who he was – how could that be?

What were they going to do with him? Was it some sort of twisted revenge for the fight in the saloon? They might hurt him. Perhaps even kill him. Why hadn't Gifford helped him instead of getting hurt himself? And where was Zachary Cobb? Oh, please let Zac come soon and rescue him.

Eleven

About an hour after he'd ridden away from the river, Cobb calmed down.

'We'd better go on back,' he said to Neil. 'There's no buffalo around here and I don't trust that boy. Who knows what he'll do all by himself?' He realized he'd acted foolishly leaving Lambert as he had.

And as soon as the camp came into view he could tell, with sinking heart, that he'd been a fool indeed and obviously left Lambert alone for far too long.

'Mr Cobb, something's wrong.'

Cobb could see that for himself. A horse was missing. So was Lambert. 'Don't say the stupid idiot has gone off by himself. He'll get lost for sure.'

'No, look.' Neil pointed at the crumpled body of Gifford, covered by a blanket. 'Surely he wouldn't attack his valet even if Gifford tried to stop him?'

'I wouldn't put anything past him.' But Cobb didn't really believe that. Clearly something had happened. What? He didn't like the look of this, not one little bit.

'Gifford's not dead, is he?'

'I hope not.'

As they dismounted by the valet they saw, with some

relief, he was alive, even trying to sit up. He had a nasty bruise on his forehead and was white beneath his sunburn. When he saw them he gave a little groan and collapsed back on the ground.

Cobb squatted down by the man and gently put his arms round him, helping him into a sitting position. 'What happened? Where's Lambert?'

'Oh my God, sir.' Tears came into Gifford's eyes. 'I tried to stop them, Mr Cobb, but I couldn't.'

Cobb glanced at Neil. 'Tried to stop who?'

'Oh, sir, three men. They had guns. They rode out of the trees.'

'Where's Lambert?'

'I don't know. They knocked me down. That's all I remember. But, oh dear me, sir, I do believe Master Lambert has been kidnapped.'

'Kidnapped?' Cobb sat back on his heels in shock. Whatever he'd feared, it wasn't that. 'What makes you think so?'

'If it was anything else, a robbery or a killing, Master Lambert or his body would surely still be here. The men wouldn't have taken him away. And Master Lambert is an obvious target. It was something Mr Hutchinson always guarded against in New York.'

Cobb thought that if someone had happened to mention it to him, he could have guarded against it here too.

'What does kidnap mean?' Neil asked.

'Someone has taken Lambert and means to ask for a ransom, money, for his safe return.'

That was if he was returned. Cobb had never been involved in a kidnapping case, but several were detailed in Mr Bellington's files and none of the victims had been recovered alive.

'And you didn't see who they were? Wouldn't recognize them again?'

'Only that they were young and rough. Oh dear me, my poor master,' Gifford moaned. 'Whatever must he be going through? They might be ill-treating him. He will be so scared. You must rescue him, you must.'

'Of course I will. Neil, you stay here with George. Get a fire going, keep him warm. I'll try to find their trail.'

'OK, be careful.'

'I believe they went across the river, sir. I seem to think I heard them splashing into the water.'

Cobb rode his horse along the bank until he found the spot where the kidnappers had entered the water. He urged his horse to follow, coming out on the opposite bank, where the trail led up into the trees. For a while it was easy to follow.

God, how could this have happened? A kidnapping! Who were the men, and how had they known it was worth them kidnapping Lambert? Maybe they had realized back in Cypress Grove, where neither Lambert, nor his companions, had made any secret of his wealth and status. Maybe they had followed him from New York, figuring it would be easier to snatch him in the empty wilderness than on that city's busy streets.

Whoever they were, whatever their motives, why hadn't he spotted them? They must have been close by, watching, to know when Lambert was on his own. But then why should he have been on the lookout for something he couldn't possibly have suspected might happen?

From past experience Cobb knew ignorance would be seen as no excuse, and he wondered what on earth Mr Bellington would have to say about him losing not just a rich client but a favourite nephew. He closed his eyes. It didn't bear thinking about.

Gifford lay propped up against a rock, a blanket over his shoulders, shivering near the fire Neil had lit.

'Here you are.' Neil handed him a cup of coffee. It was strong and bitter but at least it was hot, and the man sipped at it gratefully. Neil was relieved to see a little colour had returned to his face. 'How are you feeling now?'

'Better, sir. But, oh dear, I'm so worried about poor Master Lambert. I let him down. I'll never forgive myself if he's not recovered safely and soon.'

'It wasn't your fault.' Neil wondered at the man's devotion to Lambert when Lambert was nothing but rude to him. 'If you'd tried to do anythin' you might've been worse hurt, perhaps killed.'

Gifford shook his head. 'You don't understand, sir.'

'If anyone can get him back Mr Cobb can. He's very good at his job.' If Gifford could be loyal to Lambert then Neil could be just as loyal to Cobb.

'Bastards!' Cobb came to a halt at the river.

By good luck, good judgment or experience at fleeing chasing lawmen, the men had turned him in a complete circle. They'd backtracked, wiped out their trail, ridden amongst the rocks, maybe gone down in the river again. Cobb had no way of knowing. He was a reasonably good tracker, if he had a reasonable trail to follow. He wasn't an expert. He rode up and down the banks of the river without finding any more clues as to the men's whereabouts. By now it was almost too dark to make out anything.

As much as he didn't want to, he knew he was wasting time and ought to give up. He wasn't going to find the kidnappers now. And he ought to go back to Cypress Grove, as much as he didn't want to do that either.

There was Gifford to consider. The man didn't seem to be badly hurt but he was no longer young and he might be hurt inside. He ought to see a doctor. Quinn would have to be informed. The marshal's help sought. And – Mr Bellington would also have to be telegraphed.

Oh, hell!

'No luck?' Neil asked when Cobb returned to the camp.

'No, I lost the bastards. How's George?'

'Not so bad. With rest and time he'll be OK.'

'Unfortunately I can't allow him either one. We must start back to Cypress Grove and he'll have to ride. There's no other way to get him back.'

When told the valet sounded tired but resigned as he said, 'It's all right, sir, I understand. It's a shame you couldn't find the men but as you haven't then it's best you seek help in rescuing Lambert. How long do you think it'll take?'

'With luck we should reach town by early tomorrow morning.'

'But, sir, it took us three days to get here.'

'I know but the journey out was real slow and we had a lot of stops.'

'You don't intend to stop on the way back?' Gifford
sounded mournful.

'Not lessen we have to.'

'No one's comin after us,' Crowell said. 'We'd better
stop for the night.' It was too dark to go on and now the
sun had gone down, he was shivering with cold in his
still-wet clothes and he knew he and Lambert had to get
warm and dry. The small brush-choked clearing, sheltered all round by pine-trees, seemed an ideal spot.

As they came to a halt Crowell went over to Lambert,
heaving him off the horse so he fell to the ground with
a painful bump. Through the gag Lambert made a
muffled sound of anguish. He bent over his captive.

'If'n I take off the gag will you quit your damn moaning?'

Lambert nodded, too miserable and scared to do
anything but agree. 'What about the ropes? Will you
untie me as well?'

'I ain't that stupid.'

'I give you my word I won't try to escape.'

'Don't believe you.'

Lambert said haughtily, 'I'm a gentleman, my word is
my bond.'

'Mebbe. But you're worth too much to take any
chances over. I'll untie you when you eat not before.
Now get on up and come over to the fire.'

As Crowell helped him to his feet, Lambert stumbled. It seemed to him that every single part of his body
hurt and that he'd never get the feeling back in his
arms and legs. He was pushed over to where Norton
had started a fire. It was a relief to both young men to

74

sit down near its light and heat.

Lambert decided to risk one question. 'Why have you kidnapped me?'

'For money, kid, what else?'

'I suppose I might have known! Well, my father will pay, no doubt of that.'

'Good.'

It would have been wise for Lambert to keep quiet. Wisdom had never been one of his virtues, especially when it came to listening to his own voice and opinions.

'Don't sound so pleased. You might think yourselves clever and cunning but you'll never get away with this. My father is an extremely influential man from the east. He'll ensure the full weight of the law is brought to bear on you all. You'll never enjoy your ransom money. Instead I imagine you'll rot in jail, that is if you're not hanged.'

'Hell, don't he go on?' Hatcher said, with a grin.

'He's got to catch us first, son.'

In a sulk at being mocked Lambert lapsed into silence.

'Supper's ready,' Norton said and started to pile the food onto battered tin plates.

As he had promised Crowell untied Lambert's hands. The boy took the plate offered him. He stared at it. 'What exactly is this meant to be?'

'Beef stew.'

'Slop more like. I can't possibly eat it.'

'Then you'll have to go without. It's all there is,' Crowell said. Mind you, he thought, the kid had a point; Bruce's cooking left quite a lot to be desired.

'And you call this coffee? What I want is . . .'

But they weren't to find out what Lambert wanted because Crowell waved the bandanna in front of his face. Fearing he would be gagged again, the boy sat back, grimaced, and said no more.

As he ate, forcing the food down because he was hungry, he studied his captors. They weren't much older than him but were so different – quite ignorant with their rough way of talking and casual use of swear words, and quite common with their scruffy way of dressing. Really he should have nothing to fear from them.

Yet here he was unable to do anything. He was efficiently tied up – tied up! him! how disgusting! – and these outlaws were bristling with weapons they were probably only too willing to use. And if he did escape where would he go, what would he do? He had no idea where he was, nor in which direction Cypress Grove lay. He could ride around for days and never reach safety. And if he did try to get away and didn't succeed then these thugs could take it into their heads to punish him, to hurt him, and Lambert didn't want to risk that, for he wasn't a very brave young man.

No, he would just have to put up with the situation. For as dreadful as it was he knew he could be treated a lot worse. He was after all being given food to eat and coffee to drink, however bad it was. And being allowed to sit by the fire. With good fortune his ordeal would soon be over.

In the meantime he could content himself with imagining all the punishments he and his father would visit upon these dreadful young men.

And of course once he was free he would return

home to New York and his family to a hero's welcome, able to ask his father for whatever he wanted – a larger allowance, a good job in the bank – a vice-presidency probably – Cobb's head on a platter for allowing this to happen.

'Mick, when d'you reckon we'll reach the line shack?' Norton asked as they all lay down to sleep.

'Mid-morning,' Crowell hazarded a guess. 'It can't be far.'

'I wonder who it belongs to.'

'The MacLean family mebbe. We must be quite near their ranch.' And before his eyes closed Crowell thought about Veronica again, remembering her good looks and fresh smell, the food they'd enjoyed and the comfort of the small ranch.

He stared up at the sky, the stars were very bright. Soon they'd be two thousand dollars richer. Able to afford a ranch of their own. Please, God, he thought, this time let it work out like it should.

'Here.' Cobb handed the canteen of water to Gifford.

The man took a grateful sip. 'How much further, sir? Surely we must nearly be there by now.' He sounded very tired.

Cobb stared up at the sky. Pale streaks in the east heralded the coming of dawn. He knew he'd been pushing them hard in his anxiety to get help. As well as Gifford, Neil was pale-faced with exhaustion and the horses stood, heads drooping. Yet what else could he do? Lambert's life might depend on them acting quickly.

'It shouldn't be long now. Two, three hours.'

'Thank goodness for that.'

'Neil, when we get to Cypress Grove I want you to take Gifford to the doctor.'

Neil stretched then hugged his arms across his body, trying to keep warm. 'OK. What will you be doing?'

'Facing the music!'

Twelve

While Neil took Gifford to the doctor's, Cobb left his horse and the pack-animals at the livery-stable and made his way on foot to the hotel. He'd never been one to back down from trouble, but this was one situation he'd rather not have to face.

It was mid-morning and Quinn and Beaumont had just finished a late breakfast in an otherwise deserted dining-room. Cobb was glad. He didn't want anyone who didn't have to to hear about the kidnapping nor to witness him confessing his incompetence.

'Mr Cobb!' Quinn cried when he saw the private detective. He jumped up, napkin falling from his lap. 'What is it?' For it was obvious from Cobb's grim face that something was wrong. 'Where's Lambert?'

'You'd better sit down.'

White-faced and trembling, Quinn did so. Cobb pulled up a chair and told him and Beaumont about the kidnapping.

'Oh dear, oh my,' Beaumont kept saying, wringing his hands, but he didn't appear too worried; he seemed to find it amusing.

Quinn ran a hand over his eyes. 'But how could you allow it to happen? You were there to look after Master Lambert. We'd heard such favourable reports of your abilities and now you've let the poor boy be kidnapped! How could you?'

'I'm sorry. I really am.'

'It might not be all Mr Cobb's fault,' Beaumont pointed out. 'He could have no way of knowing, no reason to suspect, such a thing was likely.'

'Surely you must have realized someone else was out there? Following you?'

'No. If I had I'd have done something about it. Mr Quinn, Gifford said Lambert's father feared something like this might happen in New York. I suppose there were no threats, no hints it might happen here?'

'Of course not. We would have told you.'

'Nothing like it happened in New York either,' Beaumont said. 'It was simply a case of Mr Hutchinson allowing his fears over Lambert to get the better of him.'

Quinn frowned at his personal assistant. 'A rich young man like Lambert is always a target.'

'Yes, but Mr Hutchinson took quite unnecessary measures to protect his family.'

'Maybe not, now it seems Master Lambert has indeed been kidnapped!'

Beaumont fell silent, having nothing to say to that.

'So you have no idea who the kidnappers might be?'

Quinn shook his head. 'Mr Cobb, I have to agree with Beaumont that none of the Hutchinson family was ever actually threatened with kidnap. It was simply something Mr Hutchinson wisely guarded against. He would never have allowed his son to travel out west if a definite threat had been made.'

'What's surprising is why and how the kidnapping took place here,' Beaumont said.

'What do you mean?' Quinn asked.

'Well, who was there to know who Lambert was or where he was going?'

'Someone must have done.'

'Couldn't it have been a band of outlaws who simply happened to pick the right victim?' Quinn suggested but neither Cobb nor Beaumont looked convinced. 'Oh dear, Mr Cobb, whatever shall we do?'

'Mr Hutchinson will have to be told. So will Mr Bellington.'

'Naturally. Goodness me,' Quinn smacked one hand into the palm of the other, 'whatever will Mr Hutchinson do? He'll be devastated. This is an awful thing to happen. Just absolutely awful!'

When Neil arrived at the hotel, Cobb was sitting alone in the dining-room drinking a cup of hot coffee. And looking extremely unhappy.

'Hi,' he said, signalling to the waiter for some coffee for Neil. 'We're evidently too late for breakfast.'

Neil grimaced. He was hungry.

'How's George?'

'Not too bad. The doc said he had sunburn, some nasty bruises all over and a bruised rib. Nothin' that taking it easy for a few days won't cure.' Neil reached out for part of a roll left on Beaumont's plate and began to chew it. 'He thinks Gifford had a fall from a horse.'

'Good. At the moment the less people know the truth the better.'

'He's given Gifford somethin' to help him sleep and is goin' to keep him at his place 'til he wakes up. Then he can come back to his room here. What about you?'

'Don't ask.'

'Where are the two city gents?'

'Upstairs putting on their hats and coats. Even in an emergency they can't go out without 'em. Then Quinn is going to telegraph—'

'Mr Cobb! Mr Cobb!' Quinn raced into the room, Beaumont at his heels. The waiter clearing tables in the corner stopped what he was doing to gape at the man as he came to a halt, waving an envelope in the air.

'What is it?'

'I was in my room putting on my coat and when I turned round someone had slipped this under my door.'

'You didn't see who?'

'By the time I opened the door the corridor was empty.'

'Beaumont?'

The man shrugged his shoulders. 'I didn't see anyone or hear anything until Mr Quinn banged on my door.'

'Let me see.' As Quinn almost collapsed in a chair, Cobb pulled a single sheet of paper from the envelope. In an untidy sprawl of badly spelled printing, it read:

We got the kid. We wont ert him ef you do as your told. We want $10,000. Cobb to bring muney to Tylers Rocks. Put it in fork of litening blasted tree

by rocks. If you dont kid is killed. Come alone.
Dont tell no one pertikularly the marshal.

Cobb frowned.

'What's the matter?' Quinn asked. 'It just confirms what we already knew.'

'Yeah, I suppose so. Ten thousand dollars is a lot of money.'

'I'm quite sure Mr Hutchinson will believe his son is worth any amount that is demanded.' Quinn was huffy. 'At least I can include that information in my telegraph to him and hopefully receive his agreement to a bank transfer later today. Mr Cobb, you will act in this matter won't you and take the money out to this place, Tylers Rocks?'

'Do you trust me to do so?'

'Of course.'

'All right, I agree. You realize the kidnappers haven't said anything about how we get Lambert back?'

Quinn bit his lip reading the note again while Beaumont said, 'Once they've been given the money won't they leave him at these rocks?'

'Maybe. I'd be happier if the note actually said so.'

'Surely they'll keep their end of the bargain?'

'I hope so, Mr Quinn. At the moment we have no way to get in touch with or negotiate with them. We're simply expected to trust them. I don't like it.'

'What else can we do?'

'My advice would be to tell Marshal Franks. Enlist his help to set up a search. Maybe he's got an experienced tracker who could—'

'No!' Quinn interrupted, his face assuming a stubborn look. 'No! The note specifically warns us not to involve the marshal. One of the kidnappers must be here in town watching us, making sure we do what they want. I am not about to do anything that might jeopardize Lambert's safety.'

'Up to you.' Cobb agreed with a shrug.

As far as Neil was concerned Cobb had given in much too easily, so Neil thought he probably had some ideas of his own as to what he was going to do.

Evidently Quinn, not knowing the man so well, was satisfied because he said, 'Come along, Beaumont, let us go to the telegraph office. Tell poor Mr Hutchinson of this catastrophe.'

'You look worried, Mr Cobb,' Neil said once the two men had gone. 'What's wrong?'

'I'm not sure. It's that ransom note.' Cobb shook his head. 'Something's wrong about the way it was written and spelled.' He looked at his young companion. Neil couldn't read or write so it was no use asking for his opinion. 'Some of the words looked as if they were badly spelled on purpose. As if someone educated wanted to fool us into thinking it was written by someone who could barely write.'

'So who do you think did write it?'

'I don't know.'

'What are you goin' to do now?'

'There's nothing much I can do until we receive Hutchinson's approval to pay the ransom and get the money delivered to the bank here in town. Let's go see if the café will serve us something to eat.'

'Suits me.'

Cobb yawned. 'Then we can sleep for a while.'

That suited Neil too.

Thirteen

'Come on, kid, wake up.' Crowell kicked Lambert's legs. 'You are a sleepyhead, ain't you?' he added as Lambert blinked open bleary eyes and sat up. 'Here, breakfast.'

Lambert took the piece of greasy bacon and mug of coffee. He looked up at his captor. 'Please don't tie me so tightly today. Or make me ride over the back of the horse. I promise I won't try to escape.'

Mick shrugged. 'I guess you ain't got nowhere to go at that, not out here.'

All the same he wasn't about to take too many chances, so when the time came for them to ride out he tied Lambert's hands together in front of him, but not all that tightly. He didn't bother with a gag; who was there to hear? He nodded at Norton who took hold of the horse's reins so Lambert couldn't spur it away.

The line shack stood at the edge of a small meadow, about a mile or so from the old stagecoach road, which had once led from Cypress Grove up to the mining towns in the mountains. Now that the road was hardly ever used no one was likely to pass by and see people were there when they shouldn't be. It was kept in reasonably good repair, with a corral out front, in the corner of which some tools were stacked. Shutters covered the two windows and the door was securely closed.

As they neared it, Lambert forgot all about his promises. He yelled out, 'Help, help me!'

'Silly sonofabitch!' Crowell rode up close. Reaching across he swiped Lambert round the side of the head, hard enough to knock him off the horse. 'You're wasting your time. Can't you see the place is empty?'

Sulkily Lambert got to his feet, aware that Norton and Hatcher were laughing at him.

'All you've done is make it hard on your own self because now you're goin' to walk the rest of the way.' Crowell kicked the boy, propelling him forward.

Fearing more kicks and blows, Lambert started walking across the meadow. Less than halfway there he wondered why cowboys considered high-heeled boots so fashionable when they hurt like hell.

While Norton saw to the horses, Crowell took hold of Lambert's arm and opened the door, which wasn't locked.

Hatcher pulled back the shutters on the windows. The light revealed dust covering every surface. Two bunks made up with blankets and pillows stood either side of a table. In one corner was a stove and above it a shelf containing a frying pan and some chipped crockery.

'Home from home,' Hatcher said. 'We'll be OK here, Mick.'

'Not exactly what you're used to, kid, I suppose?' Crowell pushed Lambert over to one of the bunks.

'Absolutely not! Look at all this dust. Doesn't anyone ever come here and do any cleaning? And where do I wash? I feel so dirty I simply must wash and change my clothes.'

Crowell looked at Hatcher and both men burst out laughing. 'Bit of dirt and dust never did no one any harm.'

'That's obvious in your case. I'm afraid I cannot possibly stay here. This dust will make me ill.'

'Where would you like to go?'

'As far away from you three as possible.'

Crowell grinned, reluctantly admiring Lambert. The boy must be scared, wondering what would happen to him, and he was being forced to put up with things he certainly wasn't used to, and Crowell admitted he hadn't been very kind to him, but that didn't stop him speaking up for himself. Mick couldn't decide whether it was bravery or stupidity. Or perhaps, like Veronica MacLean, Lambert too didn't find them very frightening.

He gave a mocking bow. 'I'm very sorry, sir, but you've gotta suffer us and our dirty ways for a while longer. Just like we've gotta suffer you. It won't be for long then you can go back to your polite and clean society.'

'Meanwhile what the hell are we gonna do with him?' Hatcher said. 'I can't stand listening to his moaning. And we need to keep him somewhere safe where we don't have to watch him all the time and he can't get away.'

And also so that when the muffled man came with their money, Lambert didn't see him. The muffled man had made it very clear he didn't want to risk being recognized.

Norton had come in during this exchange and now from over by the space near the stove he said, 'What about down here? There's a cellar under the shack.'

When Crowell and Hatcher looked they saw a few narrow steps leading down to what was less like a cellar and more like a hole in the ground. It was probably used for storing food.

'Well, kid, you scared of the dark or spiders?' Crowell asked.

In surprise and horror, Lambert cried out, 'You can't possibly put me down there! You can't!'

'He is scared of the dark,' Hatcher jeered.

'No I'm not. Nor of spiders. But it's even dirtier down there than up here. I refuse to let you. No! How dare you even think of such a thing!'

'Oh shut up.' Crowell undid the ropes tying Lambert's wrists. 'Get on down there.' And he gave the boy a shove.

Lambert fell through the trapdoor, made a futile grab at the air and landed heavily at the bottom, yelling in fear and outrage. Before he could get up, Crowell dropped the trapdoor and secured it by pushing the table across it.

'He will be OK down there, won't he?' Hatcher asked.

None of them wanted to see Lambert, pain in the ass though he was, hurt or suffocated.

'Yeah. Look, you can see through gaps in the wood. He'll have light and air enough. And it won't be for long. Let's see if we can get the stove goin'.'

Angrily Lambert picked himself up from the floor, barely able to stand upright in the constricted space. He dusted himself down. The cellar was not really dark, bars of light coming from cracks in the wooden floor above him. The air was musty but breathable. He could hear the others talking. But how on earth was he going to stay here? Even for a short while? He was used to feather-beds, light airy rooms, hot water and warm towels whenever he demanded them.

And Gifford, who had been his valet for a long while, to look after him. He wanted Gifford now.

But thinking of Gifford for the first time since all this happened he realized that Gifford might, in fact, be dead.

Lambert slumped down against the cellar wall. He drew his knees up to his chest and put his head in his hands. He felt very scared. And alone. Although he was sure his father would tell him it wasn't a manly thing to do, he began to cry.

Marshal Franks was well aware that something was wrong. Very little happened in Cypress Grove without him being aware of it. He just didn't know exactly what. And he didn't like that.

It had something to do with those fancy folks from back east and the hard-faced private detective who'd returned to town without the young man he'd been escorting, but with someone who'd been hurt.

A flurry of activity had followed, including a visit to the telegraph office. Franks knew it would be useless to question the operator as to what any telegraphs had said. The operator had sworn an oath of secrecy, and neither bribes, threats nor anything else would make him reveal the contents of the messages that passed through his office.

Franks decided that together with Drew Patterson he would keep a very careful eye on the situation.

Fourteen

That evening, telegraphs were received in reply to those sent by Cobb and Quinn.

That from Mr Hutchinson naturally agreed to the payment of ten thousand dollars as ransom for his son.

'Mr Hutchinson will make the necessary arrangements so I can collect the money from the bank here in town tomorrow morning,' Quinn said. 'And,' he consulted the telegraph, ' he's coming out here as soon as arrangements can be made. He is, Mr Cobb, naturally most distressed and displeased.'

Leave out the distressed part and displeasure summed up Mr Bellington's attitude. His message was long, a sure indication of his state of mind for he rarely spent money if he could avoid it. He was furious, despairing and completely baffled as to how one of his best detectives could be so careless, could have bungled his assignment so badly as to lose such an important client – and a relative at that! Cobb had better retrieve Lambert safe and well – or <u>else</u>!

Red-faced Cobb stuffed the telegraph in his pocket, wanting as few people as possible to know its contents.

'You will go out to Tylers Rocks on your own, won't

you?' Quinn said anxiously. 'You won't involve the marshal?'

'Don't worry,' Cobb said.

Quinn eyed Neil doubtfully. 'What will Travis be doing?'

Cobb never liked anyone knowing all his plans and just said, 'Don't worry about Neil, I've got things for him to do in town.'

Neil said nothing. He felt sure Cobb had something more in mind. He waited to ask what it was until they were alone in the hotel bedroom.

Cobb sat down on the bed, pulling off his boots.

'Once I've left I want you to avoid Quinn and Beaumont, try to make sure no one is watching or following to see what you do, wait about ten minutes and then come after me. And, look, Neil, I don't know if the kidnapper who left the note under Quinn's door is still in town or if he's joined up with the others. Approach Tylers Rocks from the east and even if you see me don't come anywhere near me. And don't get too close to the Rocks so anyone sees you. Can you do all that?'

'Yeah,' Neil said, trying hard to take it all in. 'What then?'

'Watch out for the kidnappers. See what they look like and which direction they take. I don't know either if they'll all be at Tylers Rocks watching out for me to make sure I'm alone or whether they'll turn up after I've left the money in the tree. So you might have a long wait.'

'Do you want me to follow 'em?'

Cobb shook his head. 'No, just see which way they go.'

'What will you be doing?'

'Don't worry about me. I shan't be far away.'

'What if they've got Lambert with 'em and they leave him at the rocks?'

'Doesn't matter. Lambert is my responsibility. He's there, I'll look after him. Getting him back alive is my main concern, but I also want these bastards caught.' No one was going to best Cobb and get away with it if he could help it. 'Neil, I've got to tell you I do not like any of this. So you be careful. Don't take any chances.'

'OK.' Although he tried not to show it, Neil was frightened. Not because of any possible danger. He was scared of letting Cobb down.

Ten thousand dollars!

In crisp new bills!

They counted it out in the hotel bedroom well away from prying eyes. It was a lot of money. It looked like a lot of money, making the saddle-bags bulge.

'You know what to do, Mr Cobb?' Quinn fussed around him as they went downstairs and out into the road where Cobb's horse waited, saddled and ready to ride.

'Yeah, don't worry.'

'Nothing must go wrong.'

'It won't.'

'Please bring Master Lambert back with you.'

'I'll do my best.' Wanting to be on his way, wanting this over and done with, Cobb turned from the man and swung up into the saddle. 'Neil, I'll see you later.'

'Yeah, sure, look after yourself.'

Cobb rode out of Cypress Grove, cursing himself

because he felt nervous. Put him in any kind of fight, against any kind of outlaw, that was one thing; dealing with unseen villains, who had someone's life beside his own in their hands – that was completely different. Something he wasn't used to.

It was all very well to pay the ransom. He could understand Hutchinson doing that. But there seemed no guarantee whatsoever that the kidnappers would have Lambert with them to exchange for the money. How they were going to get Lambert back, if they were going to get him back, hadn't been mentioned. The kidnappers could just take the money and ride away. Of course, Cobb would immediately start out on their trail, but that wouldn't help Lambert.

Like he'd told Neil, he wasn't happy, and not just because everyone, including himself, thought he'd failed in his duty. There was something wrong about all this, and Cobb was even unhappier because he couldn't figure out what it was. He was afraid the hurried plans he'd made wouldn't do any good. Perhaps he should have kept Neil with him; or ordered Neil to tell Marshal Franks what was going on.

Well, it was too late for that because he was here now.

Standing all alone in the middle of the meadow, a tall outcrop of rocks, boulders and bushes, Tylers Rocks made a perfect place for an ambush.

Cobb approached the rocks cautiously. He kept a hand on his rifle, ready if necessary, to pull it out of its scabbard and dive off his horse all in one swift movement. But he saw and heard nothing, except for birds swooping among the trees.

The sycamore blasted by lightning stood all by itself

at the base of the rocks, two burnt arms reaching up into the sky.

Cobb dismounted close by and carried the saddle-bags over to it. In the fork between the tree's two arms was a deep hole. Pushing the saddle-bags into it he stepped back. The hole made a good hiding-place, as the saddle-bags couldn't be seen. At least no casual rider-by would spot them and suddenly find himself ten thousand dollars richer!

Eyes flickering round but still seeing no one, he waited for a while, in the hope that the kidnappers would appear and have Lambert with them. But in his heart he knew he was wasting his time. His experience told him he was out here all alone.

So after a few moments he re-mounted and rode back the way he'd come. A little way into the trees where he was sure he couldn't be seen, he came to a halt, dismounted again and settled down to wait.

Once Cobb had ridden away Neil told Quinn and Beaumont he had some purchases to make and hurried away, although Quinn clearly wanted to keep an eye on him. Once he was out of their sight he did his best to make sure neither they, nor anyone else, were following him. Which, he decided, with all these people around, was easier said than done, although Cobb probably wouldn't have had any difficulty.

After waiting for what he thought had to be ten minutes, he went down to the stables.

Glancing over his shoulder – good, no sign of anyone – he pushed open the door and stepped inside. And immediately sensed someone behind him. He half turned. There was the shadow of a man, arm raised. Before Neil could do anything, something hard crashed down on the back of his head.

With a little groan, Neil slumped down in the straw, unconscious before he hit the ground.

Fifteen

Never very good at waiting, Cobb managed to wait until the middle of the afternoon. In all that time he'd seen no one. He couldn't think why it was taking so long for the kidnappers to collect the ransom. Unless – their cohort in Cypress Grove was waiting for Cobb's return there before telling them it was safe to do so.

And where was Neil? Was he somewhere on the far side of Tylers Rocks also waiting for the kidnappers' appearance? Or had he failed in what he was meant to do? That seemed only too likely given the fact that Neil had little in the way of intelligence. Drat the boy! Cobb sighed. He was being unfair, taking his own shortcomings out on someone not at fault. Neil wasn't the detective. He was. It was time for him to detect.

He decided the best thing to do was ride back to town. There he could find out if Quinn had received any further communication from the kidnappers. And, whatever Quinn said, he also decided to enlist Marshal Franks' help.

Cobb stood up and mounted his horse. He was just pulling its head round in the direction of Cypress Grove when, from a long way away, he heard, carried on the wind, the faint sound of shots.

Out here shots probably weren't all that unusual – but were they something to do with Lambert?

He soon stumbled across the trail of one ridden horse. Newly made too. And so easy to follow he found it difficult to believe it was anything to do with the kidnapping. Was it Neil, disobeying his orders and actually following the kidnappers instead of reporting back to him? But that couldn't be right because there was just the one set of tracks.

Well, if it was one of the kidnappers not bothering to hide his trail because he thought no one would follow him, then he was in for an unpleasant surprise.

'Mick,' Norton called from the doorway of the line shack. 'Someone's comin'.'

Crowell and Hatcher joined him. On the far side of the meadow a rider was slowly coming towards them. Crowell raised a hand, sheltering his eyes against the afternoon sun.

'It's him,' he announced. 'And he's all muffled up again. He still doesn't want us to be able to identify him.'

'Or the kid either,' Norton added.

'Soon be over now,' Hatcher said in some relief.

In the cellar below Lambert could make out most of their conversation.

Of course it was obvious. He should have known. These men who'd snatched him had neither the brains nor the knowledge to carry out his kidnapping by themselves. Someone had told them who he was; how rich his family was, how willing his father would be to pay up. And how he was going on a hunting trip which would provide the perfect opportunity for them to seize him.

But who?

Not Mr Cobb. If Zac wanted him kidnapped he'd have done it himself. That left one of the three men who'd accompanied him from New York: Quinn, Beaumont or Gifford.

Not Gifford, surely not his loyal and trustworthy valet. He'd have no reason for it. In his heart, Lambert supposed at times he treated his manservant badly – well, all the time actually – but Gifford was well paid for his pains. Besides he'd been hurt during the attack. No, not Gifford.

But surely not Quinn either. Quinn had been a faithful member of the bank for years. Was a friend of his father's.

Beaumont then. What did he know about Alec Beaumont? Little except that he was a recent employee, only having been at the bank for six months. And there were occasions when Lambert caught the man looking at him in a strange way, almost scornfully; as if he didn't like him. Yes – Beaumont – it had to be.

What did Beaumont's arrival here mean for him? Lambert's heart beat fast with apprehension. What would happen to him now? Would he be let go? Or did Beaumont have something else in mind for him?

And what about his captors? He wasn't stupid enough not to know it would be oh-so-easy for them to take the ransom money and ride away, leaving him here, where he'd never be found, to die. He could identify them, knew their Christian names, and instead of keeping quiet had foolishly threatened them with the full weight of the law. They might decide they had nothing to lose by killing him.

He crouched and went over to the cellar steps, straining to hear.

Crowell watched as the man dismounted, leaving his horse by the corral, and walked slowly towards the hut. Mick stepped back inside and the man followed, glancing all round.

'Everything all right?'

'Yeah. No problems.'

'Where is he?'

Crowell nodded towards the trapdoor. 'Down below in the cellar.'

'Best place for the damn nuisance.'

'Have you got our money?' Norton asked from where he sat on one of the bunks.

'That's what I'm here for. To let you have your reward for your considerable efforts on my behalf.' The man reached towards his pocket.

Crowell turned away to pick up his saddle-bags in which to put the money. He heard Hatcher gasp with shock. He glanced back and his eyes widened.

For instead of pulling two thousand dollars from his pocket, the man had drawn a Colt .45.

'What the hell?'

'Jesus!' Norton cried out and went to jump up. 'No, don't!'

Things happened very quickly after that.

The man swung the gun towards Norton and fired once, twice. Both bullets caught the young man in the chest. Screaming, he was flung back down on the bunk, legs dangling lifelessly over the side.

Next, before Hatcher could move, the muffled man shot him twice in the head. Blood and brains splattered over Crowell, who cried out in horror and stepped back.

At the same time Mick reached for his gun. He might have succeeded in drawing it but even as he pulled it halfway out of its holster, Hatcher stumbled against him, knocking him off balance.

Before he could recover, Crowell heard another shot and felt a searing pain in his side. With a little cry he grabbed at the wound. He had the sensation of falling, collapsing on the floor, Hatcher slumping on top of him. Crowell tried to push his friend out of the way but pain swept over him, followed almost at once by thick blackness. He was sure he heard the muffled man laughing.

Looking at the carnage he'd caused the man re-holstered his gun. It had been so easy, but then it always was when you dealt with greedy idiots.

In the cellar, Lambert stood listening anxiously, hands clenched at his sides. What was happening? Who was firing? There were so many shots, followed by the heavy thumps of falling bodies.

The kidnappers had thought that whoever was approaching the shack had come to pay them. Instead he'd shot them! Lambert had heard the man say something but hadn't been able to make out either what it was or his identity.

Was it Mr Cobb come to rescue him? Had Cobb played a trick on them?

Suddenly all was silence.

Yet no one came to open the trapdoor.

'Help! I'm down here.'

Lambert heard someone moving around and called out again, thinking that maybe he hadn't been heard. 'I'm here. In the cellar.'

Still nothing happened. There was no more noise.

Icy coldness settled around Lambert's heart.

The person hadn't come to rescue him. Instead he'd left Lambert all alone. Left him here to die.

Sixteen

Neil groaned and opened his eyes. He wondered why his arms and legs ached and why his head hurt. And where he was.

It was dark and cold because for some reason he was lying in a small hole in the ground with several planks of wood placed across the top. He tried to move and the reason for his discomfort became apparent. He was trussed up, arms and legs tied tightly together behind his back. One side of his face felt sticky and he realized in some panic that it was dried blood.

Rolling over on to his back he looked up to try to make out where he was. He couldn't. He couldn't even tell whether it was day or night.

Where the hell was he? Why was he tied up?

Slowly it all came back to him. Someone had been waiting for him in the livery-stable. Someone who knew he was going to follow Cobb and had stopped him by hitting him on the head.

Neil thought hard about the someone's identity but it was no use. He'd caught no more than a glimpse of a shadowy figure. A man, but that was all he could say for sure.

Whoever it was must have tied him up and carried him out to this hole in the ground and left him here. And for what? Just so he couldn't help Cobb.

At that a shiver of apprehension ran down Neil's spine. Was Cobb all right, or did the kidnappers want him all alone because they meant him some harm? And what would he be thinking? At best he would believe Neil had let him down, at worst . . . well, at worst, what?

And how long would he have to wait here until he was found? Which was all he could do, for he was too efficiently tied up to be able to free himself.

Marshal Franks stretched. One o'clock. Time to set off for home and dinner.

It was a routine he followed every day at this time. And he also followed the same route: a walk round the main square, through the business district and along by the railroad tracks to his home. Where his wife would be waiting with coffee, dinner and some conversation.

Neil became more uncomfortable by the minute. He could hear the snuffling sounds of horses and thought he was at the back of the livery-stable, which made sense as his attacker wouldn't have wanted to carry him too far for fear of being seen. Did anyone come by here? Was he going to starve to death? His body need never be found.

Although surely Cobb would set up a search for him but by then it might be too late.

And what about Quinn and Beaumont . . .

What was that? A horse! One being ridden!

'Help! Help!' Neil cried as loudly as he could. His

voice sounded croaky and swallowing hard, trying to work up some saliva, he tried again. 'Help, please!'

He listened hard but there was nothing more. Had the rider heard him or gone on by?

After what seemed an eternity, during which Neil felt sure the rider was no longer there, someone called out, 'Who is it?'

'Here! Over here.'

Cautious footsteps approached and someone tripped over the planks of wood, almost falling into the hole, cursing loudly at the same time. Then the planks were pulled away and, sighing with relief, Neil made out the outline of a man, kneeling, peering down at him.

'My God, boy, what the hell's happened to you?'

'It's a long story.'

'Let's get you outta there.'

The man rolled Neil over, his hands starting to undo the knots on the ropes. The same hands grabbed at his body, pulling him out of what proved to be a shallow hole dug in the alley running along the back of the livery stable. Neil's relief at being free died a little when he saw the winking of a marshal's badge. This was going to take some explaining, and Marshal Franks didn't look the type to be fobbed off with lies.

Franks helped him into a sitting position and stared hard at him, recognizing him as having been with the party of easterners. He frowned. What was going on here?

'Well, son, I'm on my way home for hot coffee and warm pie. You look as if you could do with both. So, you can make it easy on yourself and come home with me,

tell me your long story there, or I can march you back
to the jail and you can tell me there. And let *me* tell *you*
I won't be any too pleased if I have to do that because I
too want my coffee and pie. What's it to be?'

Neil sighed. He'd had had enough experience of
lawmen, was scared enough of anyone with a badge, to
know he'd have to confess everything to Marshal
Franks, however much Cobb and the others wouldn't
like it. Might as well do it in comfort as not.

'I'll have some of that coffee, please.'

Marshal Franks stared at Neil as if he didn't believe
him. A kidnapping!

Having just enjoyed some of Mrs Franks' good cooking, they were sitting in the small, neat dining-room
overlooking the yard in front of the house, which was
surrounded by a white picket fence.

'What are you goin' to do?' Neil asked, accepting
another piece of apple pie from Mrs Franks. 'Thanks,
ma'am, it's very good.'

Franks didn't answer because he didn't know. He
knew how to deal with most things – troublesome
whores, drunken cowboys, fist fights, even shootings.
But a kidnapping, and of a rich young easterner, the
son of a bank manager, who was coming hotfoot out
here from New York, well, that was something else.

'You don't have any idea of who the kidnappers
were?'

Neil shook his head. 'No. Gifford, you know the valet
or something, said there were three of 'em. They were
young . . .'

Oh God, Franks thought, hoping it wasn't the three young men who'd caused trouble at the Deer Horn Saloon and who he'd said were probably harmless.

'. . . but he didn't have time to get a good look at 'em before he was hurt.'

'And you say Cobb should be back by now?'

'Yeah. 'Less he's following the kidnappers.' But Neil didn't sound too sure about that. 'Or lessen something's happened to him. I'm real worried.'

'It's a pity he didn't see fit to tell me what's going on. This is my town. I could have helped.'

'There's no need to take it out on Neil,' Mrs Franks said. 'It's not his fault.'

'He wanted to but Mr Quinn ordered him not to because the kidnappers wrote they'd kill Lambert if the law was involved. They might still kill him if they find out I've spoken to you.' In a very worried tone, Neil repeated his earlier question, 'Marshal, what are you gonna do?'

'First thing I'm having a talk with all these easterners and then I'm riding out to Tylers Rocks, see if I can find Cobb or this Lambert boy.'

'Can I come with you?'

'I don't see why not.'

From over by the window, Mrs Franks said, 'I don't think that's a good idea. Look at the clouds. Storm's on its way.'

'Can't we still go?' Neil asked anxiously.

'You obviously don't know what a storm in the hills is like. But we'll see. In the meantime, Neil, you'd better stay here out of sight in case you weren't meant to escape from that hole.'

107

And so Franks could keep an eye on him, because Neil might be making some of this up.

'You can stay the night too.'

And the marshal's long-suffering wife left to make up the bed in the spare room.

Much to his annoyance Franks didn't have any luck. First he went back to the livery-stable. The owner hadn't seen anything of the attack on Neil, nor had Cobb returned. And at the hotel he was told although Gifford was now back in his room he was feeling so groggy he had asked not to be disturbed. Quinn and Beaumont were also in their rooms and they too had asked not to be disturbed because they were working.

Franks could have pushed it, insisted they talk to him. He decided not to. While he didn't think it likely, supposing one of the kidnappers was still in town watching the easterners? He didn't want to do anything to put Lambert's life in danger. And from what the Travis kid said the three men didn't know anything important anyway.

He went back to his office, took Drew Patterson into his confidence, and told his deputy to patrol the area around the hotel for the rest of the afternoon and keep an eye open for Cobb's return.

'And if anything happens, anything at all, you come get me.'

By the time Franks got home the storm had broken over the mountains and the first drops of cold, heavy rain reached Cypress Grove. Turning up his collar, he looked up at the now black sky. He felt sorry for anyone caught out in it.

Seventeen

Slowly Mick Crowell regained consciousness. He opened his eyes on to horror. Hatcher lay across him, half of his face blown away, while Norton slumped, unmoving, on the bunk.

'Bruce, Bruce,' he called but without any real hope of his friend replying. 'Oh God,' he moaned. Hal and Bruce were both dead. He looked down. The left side of his shirt was soaked with blood and when he touched the wound he cried out in agony, feeling like he was on fire. 'Oh God,' he repeated, realizing that unless he got help he'd be dead too before long.

He couldn't believe any of this. One minute the three of them had been planning what to do with two thousand dollars; the next his two friends were dead and he was dying. His jaw set with anger. They'd been set up. The muffled man had used them. He'd never had any intention of paying them any money. Instead he'd shot them and left them to take the blame for the kidnapping of Lambert Hutchinson . . .

Lambert! What had happened to the kid? Was he dead too?

Below in the cellar, Lambert heard Crowell.

Somehow one of his kidnappers was still alive. He called out, 'Down here, please, let me out.'

Dizzy with pain, Crowell pushed Hatcher's body off of him, the effort almost making him pass out again. White-faced he crawled over to the trapdoor which still had the table on top of it. 'Hey, kid, you OK?'

'Yes, yes, help me. Get me out.'

Crowell slumped back against the wall, legs out in front of him, sweat beading his forehead. 'I can't,' he mumbled and closed his eyes.

'You must!' Lambert waited below, feelings of panic sweeping over him again. 'Help, help,' he called but this time there was no reply.

As he emerged from the trees, Cobb saw the line shack. He approached it cautiously, ready to fire the rifle he held across the saddle pommel. In the shade he saw four horses milling about in the corral, but no one came out to challenge him. He had a bad feeling about this, the hairs on the back of his head sticking up on end.

At the door he got off his horse and, ready for anything, stepped inside.

What he saw caused him to come to a halt in shock.

Two dead men, flies already buzzing thickly around them. Another with blood all down his side and more blood splashed across his face, laying against the far wall. Was he dead too? No! For as Cobb got closer the young man blinked open his eyes and groaned.

For the moment Cobb spared him no sympathy. Hunkering down in front of him he said, 'Where's Lambert, you sonofabitch? You've hurt him, I finish

110

what's been started here.'

Crowell looked at him with unfocused eyes before saying with an effort, 'Down there.' He fluttered a hand towards the trapdoor.

Quickly Cobb moved the table out of the way and opened the trapdoor. Fearing to find another dead body it was with an enormous sense of relief that he glimpsed movement. 'Lambert?'

'Mr Cobb! Zac!' The boy's voice was weak. Then he was rushing up the steps and flinging himself at Cobb's chest, bursting into tears.

Never comfortable with displays of emotion, Cobb paused, before reluctantly and awkwardly putting his arms round Lambert, holding him close. 'It's OK. It's over. You're safe now.'

After a while Lambert's tears dried up and he stepped away, wiping his eyes on his dirty shirt-sleeve. He stared at the room. 'Oh my God, they're dead aren't they? Oh God, I've never seen a dead body before.' He looked as if he might be sick.

Cobb gripped his arm, giving him a little shake. 'It's all right. They can't do anything more to you. I'll get you some water.'

'Where are you going?' Lambert's voice rose hysterically.

'Outside to fetch my canteen.'

'Don't leave me.' Quickly Lambert followed Cobb outside, breathing in the warm, fresh air. He took a drink of water, feeling better.

'Are you OK? They didn't hurt you?'

'I've been hurt, humiliated and half-starved.'

Cobb took little notice of Lambert's indignant reply.

As far as he could see, apart from a bruise on his cheek, a torn shirt-collar and the fact that his clothes weren't as clean and well pressed as Gifford usually kept them, Lambert seemed unhurt; phsyically anyway.

'What the hell happened in there?'

'Someone hired those men to kidnap me and then betrayed them.'

'Any idea who?'

Lambert shook his head. 'Unfortunately, no. I was locked up in that awful cellar and didn't see anyone. I didn't hear the man's voice clearly enough to make it out either. But, Zac, it must be either Quinn or most likely Beaumont.'

Cobb agreed. All along he'd had the feeling something about the kidnapping wasn't right. Now it made more sense.

'I thought I was going to die in there.'

'All right, let's talk about it later when we get back to town.'

'Are we going now?'

'Right after I've buried those two bodies.'

'Whyever are you going to do that?'

'Out of decent Christian kindness is why. Afterwards we'll start straight back to Cypress Grove. Your pa will be arriving tomorrow and you can return home to New York with him.'

Lambert looked down at the ground. 'I shan't be sorry. The West hasn't proved to be what I thought it would.'

Cobb felt sorry for the boy and his broken dreams. He'd had a bad fright and a bad time and it would take him some time to recover.

He went back into the shack, Lambert reluctantly following, trying not to look at the bodies. Cobb bent down by Crowell, who was unconscious.

'His name is Mick. He was their leader.'

'I recognize him. And the others. They were the young men at the Deer Horn Saloon.'

'Yes I know. What do you think you're doing?' Lambert added, in his old imperious tone as Cobb lifted Crowell up, carrying him over to the empty bunk.

'This man is wounded. If I don't stop the bleeding he'll die.'

Lambert muttered something about that being all right by him.

'Well, I'm not about to just let it happen. Why don't you saddle up a couple of horses? See what we can take with us.'

Cobb took off Crowell's shirt. He winced when he saw the wound because it was clear the bullet was still in there. He took off Norton's shirt and tearing it into strips used them to wipe away the blood and to tie tightly around the wound. It was all he could do.

After that he carried the two bodies outside. He was pleased to see a spade amongst the tools stacked by the corral wall. There didn't seem much point in asking Lambert for help; the boy wouldn't know one end of a spade from another.

Digging two shallow graves, Cobb rolled the bodies in them, covering both with earth and rocks in the hope that wild animals wouldn't dig them up. He had no means, or the time, to fashion crosses. But he did stop to say a few words over the dead men, repeating the only prayer he remembered from his childhood. It didn't seem right not to do at least that for them.

Lambert stood by his side and when he'd finished said, 'I wonder why the horses were left here. If anyone passed by wouldn't they think someone was using the shack and come to investigate.'

'I imagine it was easier to leave them here and hope no one would come by. Besides if there were no horses, people might ask how the three dead men inside got here.'

'I suppose so.'

'Whereas I guess it was meant to look as if they'd fallen out and shot each other.'

'And I was going to starve to death.' Lambert shuddered thinking about his narrow escape.

'Be thankful you were in the cellar and out of the way or you'd probably have been shot too.'

As they went back to the shack, Cobb looked up at the sky. It was dark, with low clouds looming over the mountain peaks. It had also turned cold.

He was very surprised when he saw Crowell had his eyes open.

'Is the bastard still alive?' Lambert asked. 'What a pity. I was hoping we'd have another body to bury.'

When Crowell saw Cobb looking at him he croaked. 'Got any water?'

Cobb held the canteen to his mouth. 'What's your name?'

'Mick Crowell.'

'How you feeling?'

'Like hell.' He looked like it too. Face blotched red and white, eyes bloodshot, sweat soaking forehead and neck.

114

'You'll soon be with a doctor.'

'Yeah and after that I'll be in jail.'

'None too soon,' Lambert muttered.

Cobb shrugged. 'You break the law, you eventually pay the price.'

'Hal? Bruce?'

'I've buried them and prayed over them too.'

'Thanks.' And Mick looked more at ease.

'We've got to be on our way. Come on.' Cobb helped him to his feet, draping a blanket over his shoulders. He half dragged, half carried him to the door. 'Hell!'

The sky was now black, more like night than day. The mountains were shrouded in rain. Could they make it back to Cypress Grove before the storm hit? Perhaps they should wait it out at the shack?

But he had a badly wounded man on his hands. And despite the fact that Crowell was an outlaw he probably wasn't that bad a one Cobb wouldn't at least try and save his life. Besides, Crowell was his only link to the man who'd planned the kidnapping. He needed him alive.

And Lambert wouldn't want to stay here – the scene of his captivity – for a moment more than necessary. Lambert needed to return to civilization, to friends and family, where he would feel safe.

Provided of course the man behind his kidnapping wasn't waiting for him.

Cobb made a decision. They'd take the chance. Start out. He heaved Crowell up on the horse.

'Oh Jesus,' Crowell groaned. He leaned forward over the saddle-horn, turning white. 'I can't do this.'

'Put up with it,' Cobb said. Mounting his own horse

he caught hold of the reins of Crowell's and with an anxious glance at the sky kicked his animal forward.

The first crack of thunder was so loud it sounded like a cannon being fired from close by.

Lambert's horse reared with fright and it was with some difficulty he stayed in the saddle. 'My God! What the hell was that?'

A bolt of lightning struck the ground, firing off sparks, and immediately another thunderbolt deafened them.

Cobb glanced round. The storm was suddenly on top of them. 'We'll have to shelter. Over there!' He pointed to an outcrop of rocks. 'Quick!'

As they neared the rocks he saw, with relief, an over-hang that would give them protection of a kind.

They made it just in time. The skies opened up and the rain came down in a drenching sheet, bouncing up from the ground, immediately forming deep puddles.

Cobb helped Crowell off the horse, laying him on the ground, where he shivered and moaned. Cobb put a slicker over him, trying to keep him warm.

Standing by Lambert, he looked out on the storm: the incessant lightning, the teeming rain and cracks of thunder. Lambert looked scared. Well he might, Cobb thought, it was enough to scare anyone. Thank God they'd been near the rocks. He didn't like to imagine what would have happened had they been caught out in the open. He realized he'd been foolish to leave the line shack where they had a roof over their heads and the warmth of the stove.

God knew how long this would last.

The Hunting Trip

*

Cobb realized they'd never make it back to town by nightfall. They'd wasted too much time sheltering from the storm. It was almost night now, and although the storm had passed by, it was still dark, still raining, the ground slippery with mud.

Lambert couldn't go on much further and Crowell certainly couldn't. He was out of it most of the time, gasping for breath, groaning when he was conscious.

They'd have to find somewhere to rest up. They were coming down out of the hills when Cobb saw the blinking of lights through the rain. They'd reached a small ranch.

'We'll stop here for the night. They'll have warmth, food and something hot to drink.'

Lambert nodded wearily, too tired to speak.

As they rode into the yard and Cobb dismounted Crowell mumbled, 'Not here, please.'

Before Cobb could ask him what he meant, if he was coherent enough to mean anything at all, the door to the house opened. Two women appeared, outlined against the light of an oil lamp behind them.

Cobb went to speak to them.

And at the same time the younger of the two demanded angrily, 'What the hell is that sonofabitch doing here?'

And Veronica MacLean raised the double-barrelled shotgun she held, finger pressing on the trigger.

Eighteen

'Hey now!' Cobb yelled. Mrs MacLean said, 'Ronny, no!' and Lambert slid off his horse, ducking out of the way.

Quickly Cobb stepped in between Veronica and Crowell. 'There's no need for that. Whatever this is about it can be sorted out later.'

'Ronny, for goodness sake put the gun down.'

'I don't see why.' Nevertheless the girl did as her mother said. 'That bastard robbed us.'

'The others didn't.'

'They might be going to.'

'I can assure you we're not,' Cobb said. 'And whatever he did in the past, Crowell can't do you any more harm. He's badly wounded . . .'

'Serve him right!'

'And me and Lambert are wet, tired and hungry.'

'See to your horses,' Mrs MacLean said. 'And then come on inside.'

'Ma!'

'Ronny, these men need our help and we must give it to them.'

Inside, the house was full of light and warmth. Between

118

them, Cobb and Lambert supported Crowell into the hall where he hung between them, head down, eyes glazed over.

'Oh my, he's in a bad way,' Mrs MacLean said, hands going to her mouth. 'He's lost a lot of blood. The poor boy.' A snort from Veronica. 'Did you shoot him?'

'No, ma'am. Is there anywhere we can take him, make him comfortable?'

'Yes, of course. My sons' bedroom. This way.' The woman hurried up the stairs, lighting the way with an oil lamp.

Veronica stamped after them as if scared they would steal anything not nailed down.

The room was small, crowded with two beds, a chair and a chest of drawers. Mrs MacLean put the lamp down on the chest and pulled the blankets off one of the beds.

'He's wet and bloody, he'll make a mess,' Veronica objected.

'Not if I undress him first.' Mrs MacLean reached down, wiping Mick's hair out of his eyes. 'And while I do that why don't you boil up a pan of water and see about some bandages?'

'Why should I?'

'Ronny, for goodness sake. Whatever will these men think? You're not usually this selfish.'

Veronica went red. 'Oh all right,' she said and left the bedroom.

'I was hoping to get him back to Cypress Grove tonight and have the doctor look at him. That's not possible now and by tomorrow he might be dead. Unless,' Cobb paused unhappily, 'the bullet is gotten out.' Which is what Mrs MacLean obviously expected him to do.

She nodded. 'Ever done something like that?'

'Once, a long time ago, when I was a deputy marshal, I had to remove a bullet from a wounded colleague. But that was easy. The bullet was in a fleshy part of his arm and he was a grizzled lawman who'd been shot before and who was conscious most of the time telling me what to do. This is different.' He shrugged, 'I've no idea how deep the bullet is in his side and he's close to dying.'

'He will die if you don't try.'

'I know.'

'I'll help you. So will Ronny despite how she's behaving. And we can have some whiskey to fortify ourselves.'

Lambert was surprised at a woman suggesting they all drink whiskey, his mother would certainly never have done so, but he said nothing. A drink was just what he could do with. On the way down the stairs, he said, 'Zac, I won't have to stay in the bedroom will I?'

'Not if you're likely to be sick.' Cobb didn't want Lambert to worry about as well as everything else. 'You stay in the kitchen. Rest. Get warm.'

Before long, much too soon for Cobb's liking, the water had boiled, towels were collected and a sharp knife sterilized by pouring boiling water over it. Mrs MacLean gave them all a whiskey and Cobb downed his in one swallow.

Crowell was shifting about in the bed. When they came in he opened his eyes, looking scared. 'Am I gonna die?'

Cobb stroked his hair. 'Not if I can help it. But I have to warn you it don't look good and it might be best if you made your peace with your God.'

'Here, son, have some whiskey.' Mrs MacLean helped Mick to take a drink.

When he'd done so, Cobb poured more of the whiskey over the wound. Crowell screamed once, long and loud, before collapsing back on the pillows.

'He's out. Ronny, hold the lamp closer so Mr Cobb can see what he's doing.'

As the girl did so, Cobb said, 'Here goes,' and without further thought plunged the knife into the wound. Crowell moaned and Mrs MacLean held him tightly. Cobb had heard of the expression 'icy sweat', now he knew what it meant. His whole body was drenched yet he felt cold at the same time.

Veronica reached over to wipe his brow as he probed deeper with the knife. 'Look, there it is!' she exclaimed.

And suddenly Cobb felt the knife touch the bullet and with a twist the slug shifted. And just as suddenly it was out!

Staggering away, Cobb sat on the other bed. 'I sure could do with some more of that whiskey, Mrs MacLean, please.' He took the bottle from her and gulped down several mouthfuls.

'Ronny, quickly, help me wash and bind the wound. You did a good job.'

'Thanks.' Cobb glanced over at Crowell, who was twitching feverishly. 'Will he live?'

'That depends how soon and easily his fever breaks. We'll know by morning. We've done all we can. Now sleep is the best thing for him and he needs to be kept warm and comfortable. And you'd better come downstairs. You and the boy look as if you could do with some supper. And me and my daughter want to hear what this is all about.'

'Exactly!' said Veronica.

As Mrs MacLean bustled round in the kitchen, heating up beef stew, and Veronica made coffee, she said, 'Mr Cobb, I don't imagine for one minute you're an outlaw like Mr Crowell up there . . .'

'Oh no, ma'am,' Zac sounded shocked. 'I'm a private detective. I work for Bellington's Detective Agency.'

Mrs MacLean hid a smile at his indignant tone. 'What me and Ronny are interested in is how you come to be in the company of one of the three young men who robbed us a few days ago and who is now badly wounded. Yet you say you didn't shoot him. What happened to the other two?'

'They're dead,' Lambert said. He had drunk more of the whiskey than perhaps was wise, and was red-faced but feeling better.

'Dead?' Veronica turned away from where she was pouring coffee into four mugs. 'How?'

'They were shot by the man who arranged my kidnapping!' There – how important that made him sound.

'Kidnapping!' Mrs MacLean exclaimed. 'My goodness me!'

She kept saying 'my goodness' all through the whole story.

'You poor boy,' she said to Lambert. 'You must have been terrified. I surely hope you weren't hurt?'

'No, not really,' Lambert admitted reluctantly, after glancing at Cobb. 'But at the time I didn't know what they might do. And if they hadn't been shot, they might have shot me rather than let me go because I could identify them.'

'I don't think they would have done anything as bad as that. They struck me as three foolish boys who were down on their luck and who didn't know any better.'

'Oh, Ma!' Veronica rolled her eyes towards the ceiling in exasperation.

'Out here people sometimes do things they don't really mean to happen. Or they're sorry for them and deserve a second chance.'

'Kidnapping is slightly more than a mistake,' Veronica pointed out.

'It seems Mr Crowell agreed to do something out of his league and he and his friends were punished for it.'

'And he'll be punished even more when he goes to prison,' Lambert added.

'The real villain is the person who arranged the kidnapping in the first place.'

Cobb nodded, agreeing with Mrs MacLean. 'Whoever he is, he's ruthless and a killer. And Lambert could still be in danger when he learns his plans have gone awry.'

'He must have collected my ransom.'

'Yeah, but you're still alive and he might fear you can identify him.'

'And neither of you have any idea who he can be?' Mrs MacLean asked.

'Only that he must be one of the three men who came West with Lambert. Perhaps Crowell will be able to tell us when, if, he wakes up.'

There didn't seem much more to say. Both Cobb and

Lambert were exhausted so while they helped Veronica wash and dry the dishes, Mrs MacLean made up beds for them on the parlour floor.

Veronica made sure all the doors and windows were shut and locked. Picking up a lamp she went upstairs. The house was quiet. Everyone else was asleep. The door to her brothers' bedroom was open and she paused to look in.

Crowell was moving his legs, trying to kick off the blankets.

Veronica tutted crossly and went inside, straightening the covers. This young man really was more trouble than he was worth! She reached over to feel his forehead. He no longer seemed as feverish as he'd been and as she stood there he opened his eyes.

'Am I dead?' he croaked. 'Are you an angel?'

'Don't be silly. You're alive and likely to stay that way. The bullet is out. Your wound isn't bleeding. Just be quiet. Try to get some sleep.'

'Will you stay with me?'

'No! Why should I?'

'Because I'm scared. I'm all alone. I've just seen my two best friends shot and killed. I'm facing life in jail.'

Veronica made a disgusted noise in her throat but all the same she sat down on the chair by the bed.

He slid his hand towards her.

Veronica clutched her own hands firmly in her lap.

'Please have some sympathy.' Tears came into Mick's eyes. 'I've got a sister at home. Suzie. About your age. I'd want her to help someone like me who's sorry for what he's done and the way his life has gone.'

Slowly the girl reached out, taking his hand. He held it, smiled, closed his eyes and slipped back to sleep. This time peacefully.

Nineteen

Much to the annoyance of others, Cobb nearly always woke up early, ready and raring to go. But, thanks to all the whiskey he'd drunk and which he wasn't used to, as well as the exhausting activities of the day before, he slept on until he heard the sounds of Mrs MacLean and Veronica moving around. Naturally Lambert was still asleep, lying on his back, snoring softly, looking very young.

And what, Cobb thought, putting his hands behind his head, was he going to do?

The most important thing was to get Lambert back to Cypress Grove. To safety. And to put his father's mind at rest.

And to see about the arrest of the person, Beaumont probably, who was behind the kidnapping.

That brought him to Mick Crowell, if the young man was still alive. If he was, would he be fit enough to travel to town? Otherwise Cobb could probably leave him here. But did he trust Mrs MacLean or would the woman, who seemed to have some romantic and foolish notions about outlaws that only a woman could possibly have, let him go?

At about the same time Crowell also woke up. He seemed to remember waking up a couple of times before along with the dawn. Then Veronica had been in the room with him, holding his hand, wiping his face, giving him some water to drink. Now he was alone. Had he imagined her being there? Being kind to him?

He couldn't remember the pain of the day before and he thought Veronica had said the bullet was out, although he couldn't remember that happening either. He felt weak as if he wouldn't be able to move far or fast. But he was going to live.

Unlike Bruce and Hal. That bastard, whoever he was, had shot them down, like they were rabid animals, not giving them a chance. It wasn't fair. It seemed like they'd finally made it good and then in the space of a few seconds it had all gone up in gunsmoke. And his two friends, friends he'd known since his childhood, argued and fought with, ridden with, shared good times and bad with, were dead.

'Oh God,' Mick moaned. They were dead. Rolling on to his stomach he buried his face in the pillow and started to cry.

And that was where Mrs MacLean, coming to see how he was, found him. Her motherly heart went out to him. Saying, 'poor boy', she gathered him up in her arms and held him while he clung to her as if by doing so he could blot out the past.

'He's awake,' Mrs MacLean announced as she came into the kitchen where the others had sat down to breakfast.

'How is he?' Cobb asked.

'The fever's gone. I think he'll be all right.'

'Good. Can he travel?'

Mrs MacLean frowned. 'I'm not sure whether he should ride a horse. That might open up his wound again.' She paused. 'Mr Cobb, do you really have to take him into town?'

'Yes,' Cobb and Lambert said together.

Mrs MacLean looked annoyed and upset and for once Veronica didn't berate her mother but said nothing, eyes fixed on her plate. Cobb decided if he should have to leave Crowell behind he would handcuff the young man to the bedpost and take the key with him.

'Zac, we are going back to Cypress Grove today aren't we?' Lambert asked anxiously.

'Yeah. And before we go I'm asking Mr Crowell what he knows about the person behind this.' Forewarned was forearmed as far as Cobb was concerned.

Crowell was sitting up in bed, resting against the pillows. He looked a great deal better this morning but was still white-faced and his eyes were red and puffy, so Cobb suspected he'd been crying.

'You going to give me any trouble?'

'No, sir, I am not.' Plucking at the blanket, Mick glanced at him and said, 'I guess I've got you to thank for saving my life.'

'Yeah, as well as Mrs MacLean and her daughter. You were in a bad way. How do you feel?'

'OK, I suppose. Sorry for what I done. Sorry about Bruce and Hal. Hell, Mr Cobb, what did we get into?'

'Why don't you tell me about it?' Cobb sat down.

'There ain't much to tell. That night we left Cypress

Grove, you know, after the fight in the saloon, we didn't ride far before we made camp. A man approached us and said he'd pay us two thousand dollars to kidnap Lambert Hutchinson, who was going on a hunting trip the next day.'

'What was he like?'

'I dunno . . . no, it's true, Mr Cobb. Both times I seen him he was so muffled up it was impossible to make out what he looked like.' Crowell smiled sadly. 'That's what we called him. The muffled man.' He paused. 'He had a strange way of talking though.'

'An eastern accent?'

'Mebbe.'

But Cobb thought Crowell had probably never heard a posh eastern accent and wouldn't know what one was like.

'And he knew the kid. In fact, he said he didn't want him kidnapped so much to get money out of his pa but to get back at Lambert for being a snot-nosed bastard and more trouble than he was worth.'

'And you went along with it?'

'Yeah but not because we really wanted to. And we did it for the money, no other reason. We were down to nothin'. It seemed so easy. No risk, all reward. I suppose we talked one another into it.' Crowell sighed.

'Then what happened? How were you going to get paid? I had to leave the ransom money at Tylers Rocks but you weren't there, were you?'

'No, sir. The muffled man said after we'd snatched the kid all he wanted us to do was take him somewhere safe where he couldn't get away. He'd come to us with our money. Well, on our way into Cypress Grove we'd passed that line shack. It seemed like a good place. Only a couple of hours ride from town and near to the old stagecoach route so it would be easy for the muffled man to find.'

Cobb sounded a bit surprised as he said, 'You didn't have to get word to him when you'd got the boy?'

Crowell shook his head. 'No, sir. He said he'd depend on you riding back to town and raising the alarm.'

Beaumont – it had to be Beaumont – who had the ransom note ready to slip under Quinn's door and so put the final part of his plan into action.

But—

'Supposing I hadn't gone back? Supposing we'd been involved in a fight and you'd shot me?' Cobb sounded as if he thought that would be most unlikely. 'Or maybe I'd have followed you instead?'

Crowell shrugged. 'I dunno. We did what the man told us is all.'

'So you're at the shack and you get your money, then what?'

'What do you mean?'

'Well, were you meant to kill Lambert?'

Crowell looked shocked. 'Of course not! We'd never have agreed to nothin' like that! We ain't . . . I ain't a killer.'

'Then what were you meant to do?'

'Wait for a while, couple of days mebbe, then let the kid go while we rode hell-for-leather out of the area. By the time the kid was found we'd be miles away and wouldn't be captured by the law.'

'And you believed all that?' Cobb asked incredulously. 'Didn't you think it even a bit strange?'

'I guess we wanted to believe it.'

'But it didn't work out like that?'

'No. The man, the bastard, wanted all four of us dead.'

'Can you tell me anything more?'

'I don't think so, no sir.' Crowell shook his head miserably. 'It was an awful thing we did and I ain't saying that just because Bruce and Hal are dead and I'm caught. I'm a thief because I was too lazy to work decent for a living but what we did to Lambert never sat right. That old guy got knocked down and hurt and I guess we treated Lambert rougher than we had a right to. I'm real ashamed of it.'

Cobb was willing to believe that the young man had been duped, had gotten in over his head but it made little difference. It didn't excuse the fact that he'd done wrong and had to be punished for it. 'I've got to take you back to Cypress Grove; you know that, don't you?'

'Yeah. I'm ready to face up to it.'

Cobb got to his feet. 'If I can arrange to borrow a buckboard from the MacLeans and put you in the back, are you all right to come in with us this morning? Or shall I leave you here and get someone to come out for you tomorrow?'

Crowell wanted to stay behind with all his heart but being a coward wasn't one of his faults. 'I'll go with you. Get it over with.' As Cobb got to the door, he added, 'Mr Cobb?'

'Yeah.'

'The kid said his father was rich and important.'

'That he is.'

'And he could get us hanged for what we did.'

'I don't think kidnapping is a hanging offence, especially when the victim is returned alive and especially in the circumstances. But, Mr Crowell, it is an offence that carries a long prison sentence.'

Crowell sighed unhappily. 'I was afraid of that.'

Twenty

Quinn and Beaumont were at the railroad station in good time for the arrival of the mid-morning train. They watched Maurice Hutchinson disembark, followed by a servant carrying two valises. He was, as usual, dressed in black, his only concession to colour being a dazzlingly white shirt and some discreet gold jewellery. Even in the circumstances, he looked smart and clean as if the dust, which covered everything else, didn't dare alight on him.

'He doesn't look very happy, does he?' Beaumont said after one look at the man's stern visage.

'Would you, if your son had been kidnapped and possibly killed?'

'I might, if my son was Lambert.'

'Beaumont, really! This is neither the time nor the place for your so called humorous remarks! Mr Hutchinson!' Quinn added, stepping forward.

'Any news?'

'I'm afraid not.'

Hutchinson's face fell. 'I hoped, trusted, that when the ransom was paid my son would be returned to me.'

'We all hoped for the same thing. But, sir, I'm sorry to say it hasn't happened.'

'Then what has happened?'

Quinn paused, looking most uncomfortable. 'I'm sorry, sir, but we don't know.'

'What do you mean?' Hutchinson clenched his hands by his sides to stop himself from clutching at the other man's coat.

'Mr Cobb hasn't yet returned from leaving here with the ransom money.'

'Why not? He went as soon as possible didn't he?'

'Yes sir, yesterday morning.'

'And he's not back by now?'

'No, sir.'

Hutchinson's eyes narrowed. 'You mean you let him leave here with the money on his own? One of you didn't think it wise to go with him?'

'Well, no, sir. You see the ransom note specifically said he was to go alone. And, well, I believed him trustworthy.' Quinn paused then added in the hope of saving himself, 'According to you he came most highly recommended by Mr Bellington.'

'I would have thought that even you, Quinn, might have wondered if anyone would be trustworthy with ten thousand dollars of someone else's money in their hands.'

Quinn reddened.

'If anything has happened to my son through your foolish mistake . . .' The man left his threat unsaid but Quinn was in no doubt that heads would roll and more than his job at the bank was at stake.

'What do you want to do, sir?' Beaumont asked,

trying to deflect some of Hutchinson's anger away from Quinn.

'I shall see the marshal.' Hutchinson caught the look that passed between the two men. 'I presume he has been told.'

'Well, er, no, sir.'

'Whyever not?'

'The note . . .' Quinn began.

'Oh damn the note! The marshal must be informed at once and his help sought.'

Quinn coughed uncomfortably. 'That won't be possible.'

'For God's sake!' Hutchinson yelled, losing his grip on his temper. 'What are you saying now?'

'He's left town too, along with Mr Cobb's assistant.'

Hutchinson followed the two men down the road towards the hotel. His head was swimming and he felt sick with worry.

Hearing about Lambert's kidnapping, having to tell his wife, had been bad enough; his worst nightmare come true. But he'd been certain that once he arranged for the ransom money to be sent to Cypress Grove and once that ransom was paid, then Lambert would be returned to him, safe and hopefully unharmed after his ordeal. For some reason that hadn't happened and not only had Cobb disappeared, so seemingly had the town marshal and Cobb's assistant.

What did it all mean? Bellington said Zachary Cobb was a good man; Hutchinson would never have let his son go off hunting with just anyone. But was he part of all this? Where was he otherwise? Or did it have something to do with the missing, the stolen, money from the bank, the culprit for which had not yet been found?

What was he going to do? What could he do?

The rain had eased up during the night, the sky again blue, the sun warm, but the ground was still muddy.

'And any tracks made yesterday have been washed away,' Marshal Franks said gloomily as he surveyed the churned-up meadow around Tylers Rocks.

Neil sighed, seeing the man was right. He could also see that no one was here; not Cobb, not Lambert, not even Cobb's body. But if the man wasn't dead then where had he gone?

Franks jigged his horse forward and rode up to the sycamore tree. 'The money's not here!'

'Then where's Lambert? Where's Mr Cobb?'

Franks put a hand on the neck of Neil's horse. 'Neil, you don't think that, well, Cobb took the money himself?'

'No!' Neil exclaimed. 'I ain't known Mr Cobb very long but the one thing I do know about him . . .' (apart from his quick temper and bad moods, he thought) '. . . is he's completely honest. He'd never do anythin' like that.'

'All right, all right.' Franks took off his hat and scratched his head. 'Well, I suppose we'd better explore the Rocks properly, make sure no one is here. And although there ain't no tracks to follow perhaps we can spend an hour or two riding round. Not far. Not for long either.'

Neil shivered. 'You think both Lambert and Mr Cobb are dead don't you?'

'It's beginning to look that way, son.'

Hutchinson pushed his plate away from him, food barely touched. He scowled at Quinn, who had just returned from speaking to Deputy Patterson.

Holding his hat, Quinn remained standing. You only sat in Hutchinson's presence when he asked you to and, still annoyed with Quinn, he hadn't asked. 'The deputy admitted that Marshal Franks has gone out to look for Mr Cobb.'

'How did he find out about the kidnapping if you didn't tell him?'

'I can only imagine that Travis, Mr Cobb's assistant, told him.'

'Why should he do that?'

Quinn shrugged. 'I don't know, sir.'

'It really is too bad.' Hutchinson wiped his mouth with his napkin. 'The matter has been handled more than badly. I would have thought I could rely on you to do better, especially as it's all so serious.'

'Yes, sir. I'm sorry, sir. And the worst of it is there's nothing we can do but wait.'

'Wait!' Hutchinson exclaimed. 'Wait? I didn't get where I am today through waiting.'

'But, sir, what else can we do? We can't go out searching for Master Lambert nor . . .'

'I don't intend to. I shall enlist the help of the army. They'll have, what are they called, Indian trackers, who are able to follow sign or whatever it is they do. If I haven't heard any more by the time I've finished my lunch I shall send a telegraph to the nearest fort asking the commanding officer to send a troop of cavalry and a tracker to meet me here.'

'I'm not sure the army will help in a civilian matter.'

'My dear Quinn, the army, like everyone else, will do whatever I and my money orders them to.'

'Yes, sir.'

Twenty-one

Dressed in some of Mr MacLean's old clothes, because his had been ruined by blood, Crowell was laid out in the back of the wagon.

To Cobb's surprise, Veronica insisted on driving it into Cypress Grove. For some reason she had gone from wanting to shoot Crowell to having the same silly notions about him as her mother. And just as surprising, Mrs MacLean didn't seem to object. But then Cobb had long since given up trying to fathom out how women thought or felt.

Waved off by Mrs MacLean, they started out for the town, reaching it in the middle of the afternoon.

'I've never been so pleased to see anywhere in all my life,' Lambert announced. 'At times I didn't think I'd ever get back to civilization.'

'Remember what I said,' Cobb warned. 'Beaumont is still here.' But it was obvious to him that in his excitement Lambert wasn't listening.

'I only hope my father is here by now.'

So did Cobb. That would mean he could hand responsibility for Lambert over to him.

As they entered the town, Cobb wondered what it

was best to do. Should he go straightaway to Marshal Franks, report what had happened and seek his help? Or go to the hotel, which was the most likely place to find Maurice Hutchinson? He decided on the latter. He could handle Beaumont, and Crowell, without any help and it would be best to let Lambert's father know as soon as possible that his son was alive and safe.

He saw he'd made the right decision when they stopped outside the Cypress Cattlemen's Hotel. The law had come to him. For the deputy was standing on the porch and he quickly walked towards them, hand resting on the butt of his gun, ready for trouble.

And as Cobb and Veronica helped Crowell out of the wagon, the door opened and Hutchinson rushed out.

'Lambert! Lambert!'

'Papa!'

Father and son flung themselves into each other's arms and hugged tightly.

'Oh,' Veronica said, wiping tears from her eyes.

'Thank God,' Hutchinson pushed his son away and stared at him. 'You're safe! Thank God.'

'Oh, Papa, I'm so glad to see you.' And Lambert hugged his father again. 'I was so scared.'

'You Cobb?' Drew Patterson asked.

'Yeah.'

At that Hutchinson stepped away from Lambert even while keeping a hold on his arm, as if he didn't want to let him go. He growled, 'So you're Cobb?'

'He saved my life.'

'Did he?' Hutchinson immediately forgot all his suspicions of the private detective and how he intended to reprimand him for allowing Lambert to be kidnapped. He shook Cobb's hand. 'How can I ever thank you?'

'Just doing my job.' Cobb felt a bit embarrassed.

'And this is Veronica MacLean. She and her mother provided us with hospitality last night.'

'Very kind, Miss MacLean. I must reward you.'

'There's no need, sir. We would have done the same for anyone in trouble.'

'No, I insist. And,' Hutchinson looked with distaste at Crowell, 'who is this?'

'He's one of my kidnappers.'

'*What!*' Hutchinson roared, while Patterson half pulled his gun from its holster.

'I'm dead for sure,' Crowell muttered, while Veronica clasped his hand tightly.

'My God!' Hutchinson went very red. 'I'll kill the bastard!'

'No,' Cobb said quickly and stepped between them. 'No. Because he's not the one you really want.'

'What do you mean?'

'It seems Alec Beaumont was behind it all.'

Hutchinson looked and sounded bewildered. 'I . . . I don't understand. Beaumont? What has he to do with it?'

The man wondered whether it was possible that Beaumont was the thief? Surely the young man had neither the brains nor the opportunity to have stolen so much of the bank's money and get away with it? Of course, the thefts and the kidnapping need not be connected, although he was sure they were.

'It's true, Papa.' Lambert glanced at Crowell. 'As much as I want this bastard punished for all he did,

141

what he put me through, in the end he was almost as much a victim as me.'

'Then let us speak to Beaumont.' If there was something to be done Hutchinson wanted to do it straightaway. 'See what he has to say for himself.' He paused.

'What's the matter?' Cobb asked.

'Well, now, come to think of it I haven't seen Beaumont since before lunch. Quinn neither after he returned from seeing the deputy here.'

'We'd better find them both.'

'Exactly, Mr Cobb!'

'By the way, have you seen Neil Travis, my, er, assistant?'

'No.'

Cobb's anger – where was the boy? – was quickly replaced by apprehension – where could he be?

'He's gone out with Marshal Franks,' Patterson said.

'He has?' Cobb was surprised, knowing how Neil felt about the law and lawmen.

'Yeah, they're looking for you.'

'Oh hell! Deputy?'

'Drew Patterson, sir.'

'All right, Drew, you stay here with Crowell, keep an eye on him while we find Beaumont.' Cobb looked at Mick, rather amused to see that he and Veronica remained holding hands. 'He won't cause you any trouble.'

'OK, sir. Come on you two let's wait inside, away from prying eyes.'

The clerk stared at their intrusion in open-mouthed surprise and horror. What was going on in his hotel? What would this do for its reputation? He didn't dare object because Mr Hutchinson was just about the richest man who had ever stayed there. Instead, without a word, he handed Cobb the pass key to the bedrooms and watched as he, followed by the two Hutchinsons, made for the stairs.

Drawing his gun, Cobb paused at the top. 'You two wait here. I don't want you hurt.' Cautiously he walked down the corridor, glad for its thick carpet muffling his footsteps.

The door to the room was unlocked. And Beaumont was inside. Sprawled across the bed, his throat cut, blood everywhere, staining sheets and pillows.

'My God!' Cobb exclaimed in surprise. He went over to the young man to confirm what he already knew: that he was dead. Beaumont's body was cold. He must have been killed some time ago, probably before lunch. But who by? And if he wasn't Crowell's muffled man then who was?

Still holding his gun and aware of Hutchinson and Lambert watching him curiously, Cobb went to Quinn's room across the hallway. He wasn't in there. In fact, it looked as if he'd left in a hurry. For while his valise was gone, some of his clothes remained behind.

Holstering his gun, Zac walked back to where the Hutchinsons waited for him.

'I was wrong. It was Quinn. He's gone and before he left he killed Beaumont.'

'What?' Hutchinson cried in horror, staggering backwards. 'I don't believe it. Not Quinn. Why, I've known him for years.'

'He's already killed two men, why not a third?'

'But why should he kill Beaumont?' Lambert asked.

'Because either Beaumont was in it with him and Quinn didn't want to share the money. Or because he wasn't but found out what Quinn was up to and so had to be silenced. I'd say it was probably the latter. I doubt if Quinn would have trusted a man he'd only known a few months with something like kidnapping his boss's son.'

'How did Beaumont find out?'

Cobb shrugged. 'It must have taken Quinn some time when he rode to the line shack and back. Perhaps Beaumont missed him.'

'I can't believe it,' Hutchinson said in a dazed tone. 'Why? Why would Quinn of all people do something like this?'

Cobb shrugged again. 'For the money.'

'If he was having financial difficulties why didn't he come to me and ask for my help?'

'Because, Papa, would you really have given it to him?'

Hutchinson went red. He turned to Cobb. 'He mustn't be allowed to get away with this.'

'Don't worry, he won't. I'll go with Patterson and Crowell down to the jailhouse, see Crowell locked up and then me and the deputy'll look for Quinn. He can't have gotten far.'

'And us?'

'You stay here. And watch yourselves. I doubt if Quinn will return to the hotel, he's out there and running, but . . . well . . . I've been wrong before.' Cobb didn't like admitting that but it seemed as far as this kidnapping went he'd been wrong about almost everything.

As they started down the stairs, Drew Patterson appeared at the bottom. He waved his arm. 'Mr Cobb! Mr Cobb!'

'What is it?' Don't say Crowell had broken his word and escaped.

'It's the afternoon train west. I've just heard its whistle. I reckon if anyone's trying to get away they might catch that train.'

'Yeah! Quick!' Cobb bounded down the stairs two at a time, looking over his shoulder at the same time to yell at Hutchinson. 'Stay with Crowell!'

Then he was following Patterson out of the hotel. And both lawmen took off at the run for the train station.

Twenty-two

Watched by curious townspeople, Cobb and Patterson raced through the streets. They reached the station just as the train pulled to a halt with another wail of its whistle and a blast of steam.

'Can you see him?' Cobb asked, the steam obscuring his vision.

'No. Yeah. There he is!' Patterson pointed towards the ticket office.

And Cobb suddenly saw the black-suited man, valise at his feet, a canvas bag clutched to his chest, skulking by the office wall. He drew his gun.

And at the same time Quinn saw him. The man's face fell in dismay. He made a sudden dash for the train, knocking into a man and woman as he did so.

'Stop!' Cobb yelled. He fired once into the air in warning.

Shocked cries and screams of other passengers echoed round the platform. The guard leapt for safety. The couple Quinn had knocked aside flung themselves to the ground, the man putting an arm about the woman. People on the train stared open-mouthed from the windows.

Quinn jumped towards the door of the nearest carriage, grabbing at the rail.

'Give it up!'

For a moment Cobb believed the man would do so. It must be obvious to him that even if he succeeded in getting on the train it wouldn't go anywhere until the shooting was sorted out. He was faced with two men, guns already out and pointed at him. Then a look of desperation came into his eyes. He reached into the bag he still held and came up with a pistol.

'Don't be stupid,' Cobb said.

Quinn fired. Once, twice.

Cobb dodged out of the way, bullets whistling by him. He was aware of Patterson diving for the cover of the ticket office. Before Quinn could fire again, which he was about to do, left with no choice, Cobb pulled the trigger. Quinn might have missed. Cobb didn't. The bullet took the man full in the chest.

With a surprised gasp, Quinn put a hand to the wound, his hand coming away all bloody. With a little cry he lost his grip on the rail and fell to the platform. At the same time he let go of the canvas bag and it landed on the ground nearby. It opened and from it spilled a number of dollar bills, some of them fluttering away in the breeze, the rest landing about his body.

Marshal Franks heard the shots and came to a halt. 'What the hell?'

Neil glanced at him. 'They came from the direction of the train station.'

'Let's see.' Franks kicked his horse's side. With a squeal it broke into a gallop.

Neil followed, his heart beating fast.

'That was shots,' Veronica said, getting up and going over to the hotel door.

'I hope Mr Cobb is all right,' Crowell said, fidgeting about in the chair.

'Whether he is or not is nothing to do with you,' Hutchinson told him. 'We must all wait here like he told us.' He was white-faced with worry. He couldn't understand why any of this was happening. He allowed himself a moment of sympathy for Quinn. The man must have been desperate to do what he did. And Hutchinson wondered if some of it was his fault for his unbending, stern attitude, even with those he considered friends.

'Drew, keep these people away.'

'All right, folks, there ain't nothin' to see. Nothin' to steal either. The money ain't yours.'

Still holding his gun, Cobb approached Quinn. The man lay on his back, arms outflung. Cobb bent down by him.

Quinn grimaced with pain. 'Jesus, it hurts. Tell Mr Hutchinson I'm sorry. Gambling debts, you know.'

Before Cobb could ask him any more, the man made a rattling noise in his throat, his eyes rolled up in his head and he was dead.

At the same time Franks flung himself off his horse and ran along the platform to where the crowd was gathered. 'What the hell is going on here?'

'Marshal.' Patterson was relieved to see his boss. This was all getting a bit much for him.

'Mr Cobb! Mr Cobb!'

Zac looked up to see Neil.

'Thank God you're OK. I was real worried about you,' Neil said. From the look on Cobb's face, he thought Cobb didn't feel the same way about him; he'd obviously done something wrong – again. 'Is he the kidnapper?' He looked down at the dead man.

'Yeah.'

Franks said, 'Drew, get these people to move on. Get 'em on the train or something. Has anyone gone for the doctor?'

'It's too late for that,' Cobb said, getting to his feet and holstering his gun.

'The undertaker then.'

'There's another dead man at the hotel as well.'

'Christ! What's been going on here?'

'I think I owe you an explanation.'

'You surely do, Mr Cobb. Although Neil has told me most of it.'

'So I believe.' Cobb scowled at Neil.

'And a good thing too! Have you recovered the boy?'

'Yeah, he's at the hotel. Along with another of the kidnappers, the other two being dead.'

Franks was looking more and more put out. 'We'd better go to the hotel then. Sort this out there! Drew, can you handle things here?'

'Yeah, Marshal.'

'Let's go then.'

'Well, Neil, what exactly happened to you that you went missing?' Cobb asked as they started down the street.

'He was knocked out and tied up,' Franks paused to

149

say. He jabbed a finger into Cobb's chest. 'And if you'd confided in me from the start he might well not have been and, in fact, most of this could have been sorted out without all this trouble!'

Franks was hardly any more pleased when he returned to the hotel and was faced with a barrage of questions and information. But at last by making everyone shut up except to tell him their own story, he grasped everything more or less to his own satisfaction.

'Umm, well, I guess I'll need to hear this all over again come morning when everyone has calmed down,' he said. 'In the meantime, you,' he pointed at Crowell, 'come along down to the jail with me. No, Miss MacLean, there's really no need for you to come as well. You should go home.'

Franks couldn't understand why the girl was behaving like she was. He liked Veronica. Usually she was a sensible girl and her mother was a sensible woman. Neither seemed to be very sensible at the moment: what with Mrs MacLean allowing her daughter to come into town with an outlaw and Veronica holding that outlaw's hand! Wait until he told Mrs Franks.

Veronica clutched at Crowell's arm, unwilling to let him go, 'I'll come and see you tomorrow.'

Crowell kissed the girl gently on the cheek. 'I won't ever forget you.'

'Oh, for God's sake, come on!' Franks pulled Crowell away.

'Master Lambert.' Behind them Gifford appeared at the top of the stairs.

'Gifford! Gifford, old boy!'

'Master Lambert, thank God you're safe. I was so worried about you.'

Crowell stopped, resisting Franks' pull on his arm. He turned round and looked at the valet in surprise. Surely it wasn't possible ... not someone like that, plump, old, dressed in suit and shoes.

'Come on,' Franks urged.

'No, no, wait a minute.' Yet, thinking about it, the man had been short and quite fat.

'What is it?' Veronica asked.

Gifford limped to the bottom of the stairs. 'I thought I'd never see you again.'

There was no mistake.

'It's him!' Crowell cried. 'He's the muffled man!'

Everything and everyone came to a halt.

Except for Gifford. From somewhere about his coat he drew a gun, pointed it at Lambert and squeezed the trigger.

Twenty-three

There was no way he could miss.

Veronica screamed. Nearest to her, Cobb pushed her out of the way while with another shove he sent Hutchinson sprawling across one of the chairs. Neil ducked behind another chair, reaching for his gun. Franks let go of Crowell, pulling out his own weapon.

They would be too late.

Lambert was left all alone, facing Gifford.

'Look out!' Crowell yelled. He flung himself at the boy and they went down in a sprawl of arms and legs. And the bullet that would have killed Lambert merely grazed his arm.

And then it was too late for Gifford.

Even as he went to fire again he found himself facing the guns of Neil, Franks and Cobb. Unlike Quinn, he gave up, immediately throwing the gun to the floor and raising his arms.

Cobb hurried forward, kicking the Colt out of Gifford's reach while Franks put handcuffs on the man, securing his hands behind his back. Slowly Hutchinson got shakily to his feet and Veronica, trembling herself, went to help him.

'Is everyone all right?' Cobb asked, with a quick look round.

'We're all OK,' Neil replied. 'The bullet didn't come close.'

'Lambert! Lambert!' Hutchinson cried, going over to his son who, together with Crowell, was just getting up from the floor. 'Oh, you're hurt!' he added as he saw blood on the boy's sleeve.

'It's not much. It doesn't hurt. He missed.' Lambert looked at Crowell. 'Thanks to you.'

'You saved my son's life!' Hutchinson caught hold of Crowell's hand, shaking it heartily.

Crowell shrugged. 'That sonofabitch was the one paid us to kidnap Lambert. He killed my two friends.'

Everyone's attention turned to Gifford. Somehow he didn't seem quite so old or plump any more, no longer a figure of fun or disrespect. Sneering he said to Crowell, 'Thought you were dead. I suppose I should have made sure. You too,' he added, looking with loathing at Lambert.

'But why?' Lambert asked, near to tears.

'You need to ask? After all your insults. All your orders. With never a word of thanks. I bet you didn't even think of asking how I was. No, I thought not!' he added as Lambert blushed. 'You spoilt brat.'

Lambert stepped back, shocked and upset. Bad enough to be kidnapped. Worse when he found out someone he knew had arranged it. And now much much worse when that person was Gifford, his faithful valet, to learn the man had done it for the way he was treated.

'But then you're all the same. All I had to do was

pretend I'd been hurt during the kidnap and was recovering in my room because I knew none of you would bother to come and see how I was. Out of sight. Out of mind. Well, poor Beaumont did and so Beaumont had to die.'

'What about Quinn?' Cobb said.

'Oh, that sorry bastard did it for the money. He's been stealing from the bank for months. I found that out after he drank too much one night and confessed. It was easy to play on his greed and fear and demand his help. But I did it for revenge. I did all the shooting and killing, knocked you out too,' he added, looking at Neil. 'Quinn wrote the ransom note and pretended to put it under his own door.'

'But how? I mean, you can't ride or shoot.' Hutchinson sounded puzzled as well as angry.

Gifford laughed, genuinely amused. 'Well, you see, Mr Hutchinson, back home in England I was the third son of a lord. I grew up with horses and guns. Unfortunately I got into trouble, purely of my own making I admit, and fled to America. Where even more unfortunately I was employed by you to babysit your snot-nosed baby. One thing, you were both easy to fool, and Quinn wasn't the only one stealing from you.'

'Supposing Crowell and his friends hadn't come along?' Cobb asked. 'What would you have done then?'

'Oh, that was just a piece of luck. Me and Quinn were on the look out for any suitable stupid thugs we could pay to kidnap Lambert. In New York or here. Although what happened wasn't quite the plan we had in mind, in the event it was all so easy. You all did exactly what you were meant to.'

'You let Quinn go off with all the money?'

'Well, Mr Cobb, like I said, I wasn't really interested in the money, only in getting my own back. And, well, I thought if Quinn disappeared with all the money he'd get all the blame.'

Red-faced, Hutchinson said angrily, 'But it didn't work out like that and now you're going to hang.'

Gifford smiled. 'Believe me, seeing Lambert's scared face and hearing him pleading to be let go makes even that worthwhile!'

'Well, that was a strange business wasn't it?' Franks downed half of his beer. He, Cobb and Neil were enjoying a drink or two in the Deer Horn Saloon. 'I ain't sorry to see the end of it.'

'Me neither,' Cobb agreed with a heartfelt sigh. 'I never wanted the job in the first place and it all turned out much worse than I could ever have imagined.'

'I wonder if all that happened will do Lambert any good?'

It seemed to Cobb they should all have learnt something from what had happened, for none of them had come out from it well. Because Gifford was right – once back in Cypress Grove, no one, not Quinn, not him, not even Neil, had bothered to go and see how the man was. They'd treated him like the servant he was. He glanced at Neil, thinking maybe he ought to treat the boy better than he did, wondering if Neil resented him, but doubting he could. He was entrenched in his ways as much as Lambert.

He said, 'For a while maybe. But not for long. He's

too spoilt and pampered. Too stupid. Too used to getting his own way.'

Franks' eyes darkened. 'He ain't the only one.'

'What do you mean?'

'Mr Hutchinson wants me to let Mick Crowell go.'

'Whatever for?'

'Because he saved Lambert's life. Hutchinson seems to think his money can persuade any place else Crowell is wanted to forget about him.' Franks shrugged. 'I don't like rich easterners coming into my town telling me what to do, but mebbe he's right. Money talks all over. And many a young man has gone off the rails, been sorry and only needed a helping hand to follow a lawful path.' He thought Neil probably came into that category, especially when Neil refused to meet his eyes.

'And Mrs MacLean and Veronica could provide that helping hand?'

Franks smiled. 'Believe me, Mr Cobb, the MacLean women run that ranch and their men with an iron hand. Crowell goes out there, he'll soon find he won't have the opportunity to get into any more trouble!'

Cobb sighed. He didn't like to see outlaws getting away with their misdeeds, whatever the circumstances. Nor did Mr Bellington. On the other hand he was just glad this assignment was over and that come morning he could say goodbye to the troublesome Hutchinsons, father and son, and be on his way.

'Neil, how about getting three more beers?'

'All right.' Neil was also glad to be leaving Cypress Grove behind; the Hutchinsons hadn't been his kind of people, their way of life not his. And thankfully it seemed Cobb had forgotten to be angry with him for confessing everything to the marshal.

'Then we'll call it a night. We've got an early start tomorrow. The train leaves at eight.'

Come to think of it, if the past was anything to go by, neither Hutchinson would be up in time for him to say goodbye to!